Early Daze

JENNIFER GILBY ROBERTS

ISBN: 1497450950
ISBN-13: 978-1497450950

For all the neonatal staff at James Cook University Hospital, Middlesbrough and the Friarage Hospital, Northallerton.

Thank you to my betareaders Mark, Anna, Becky, Alexx, Christie and Paulina, and my proofreaders Anna, Lisa, Angie, Kiarah, Cat, Julie, Cathy and Kim.

Chapter 1

I had a baby yesterday. I know, one born every minute. Except I had only been pregnant for six months. That's not so common. And she only weighs 2lb 3oz. That's less than 1kg.

Supposedly, every mother thinks her baby is beautiful. I don't even think mine looks like a baby. Not a human one, anyway. She looks a lot like an alien. Her head is too big for her body. Her eyes are sealed shut, and her little face is all scrunched up, making her look like she's got eyebrows like Spock. Her skin is red and shiny, like raw beef. And there's a tube down her throat to help her breathe. Sorry to shock you, but that's how it is. I bet you've never seen *that* in a formula advert.

The first time I saw her, I wanted to run away. The doctors were talking, but all I could do was cry. The nurse tried to get me to put my hand over the baby, but I was too afraid. I was utterly convinced that she was too small to live.

I think I'm going to call her Samantha. We were waiting to see what name she looked like, but I can't very well call her ET.

I suppose I could do something with initials.

Forgive me if I sound flippant. I'm not heartless; I'm in shock.

I'm sure that this is all a dream anyway. I still feel pregnant; I still look pregnant. There's no baby in a cot beside my hospital bed. For that matter, there's no cot.

This *has* to be a dream.

My fiancé, Ryan, arrives while I'm expressing milk, sat on the bed in my 'side ward' (aka private room), in my pyjamas. Samantha can't breastfeed. One, because her mouth is full. Two, at this stage, she can't coordinate eating and breathing. Which is a bit of a problem. So, if I want her to have my milk, I have to get it out manually. This soon after the birth, I'm only making a small amount of colostrum – not enough to use the pump. I squeeze out the drops, essentially by kneading my breasts like dough, and then pick them up using an oral syringe. It's a long and fiddly process that yields a millilitre or two of milk. I can't recommend it as a feeding method.

Ryan wanders around the room while I wearily manhandle myself. I've done this every two hours since I gave birth and I'm worn out. It must be bad enough breastfeeding, but at least then you have an actual baby to hold instead of a 1ml syringe.

'Can you help me?' I ask, struggling to pick up the drops, as well as massage.

He looks like I've asked him to dress up in my clothes. 'Don't you want me to get a nurse, Jess? Or... your mum and sister will be here soon.'

I suppress a shudder at the thought of doing this in front of my sister. I do *not* need to hear her criticising my milk production, the size/colour of my nipples, the design of my pyjamas, etc., etc., etc.

'Ryan, you've seen my breasts before and they haven't.

Or, at least, not since I was a kid. And the nurses are busy.'

He shifts awkwardly. 'I know, but...'

I sigh.

'Ryan!' I say, as firmly as I can find the energy for. 'Sit down, take this syringe and pick up the drops as I squeeze them out. Or I'll... name the baby after your mother.'

Ryan's mother's name is Petunia Prudence. And it suits her perfectly.

He flinches. 'Right then.'

He sits down and tries to accomplish the difficult task of picking up drops without actually looking at what he's doing. Then the nurse comes in, and he *hides the syringe* like he's doing something wrong.

'Morning,' she says cheerfully, 'are you experiencing any pain?'

Only one in the neck.

The Neonatal Intensive Care Unit (NICU) - Samantha's new home - is a windowless room, brightly lit and hot, with about ten incubators plus monitors round a central desk. An incubator is a large, clear plastic box on a stand, with portholes in the sides for access. Like the things they use for hatching chicken eggs, only without the infra-red light. There are nurses, doctors and other parents - plus visitors - about all the time, and there is a constant beeping from all sides.

Coming in, we have to wash our hands and wrists thoroughly. All parents, doctors and nurses have to wash their hands on entry, even if they've popped out for two seconds and haven't touched anything. I suspect it's something that will get old very quickly. I always thought I knew how to do this, but no. There are instructions by the sink, like we're in kindergarten.

Only when we're clean are we allowed to see our baby, installed at the back of the room in Bay 4 with the octopus sign. At least it isn't a monkey.

Ryan is shifting from one foot to the other, like he's got pins and needles in his feet. He looks around the room - far too fast to see anything. Eventually, his gaze settles on Samantha. 'What is that?!' he says, sounding horror struck. 'It looks like tar.'

The stuff on Samantha's nappy does indeed look like tar, although where it's smeared it looks green rather than brown. I'm suddenly very glad I read ahead in the baby book, because it looks like she's pooped algae. I know she's been floating around in fluid for the last six months, but even so.

'Meconium,' I say confidently. 'Her first poo. It's normal. They won't always look like that.'

Ryan looks somewhat relieved. 'Good, because there is no way I'm touching that stuff.'

'It's no worse than engine oil.'

'Engine oil hasn't come out of someone's bottom.'

I must concede that point.

'There's going to be a lot of nasty things coming out of her that need cleaning up,' I say.

He shifts. 'Yeah, but you'll do most of that, won't you?'

For a minute, I'm not sure I heard that.

'I beg your pardon?'

'Well, I'll be at work, won't I?'

Oh. I guess that's true.

'But when you're at home, you'll be helping.'

'Well, since you're insisting on living at your mum's

until we get married, and we haven't even set a date, I won't get much of a chance.'

He sounds slightly bitter. This has become a bit of a problem. I have pointed out that if he hadn't got me pregnant before we got married, then we wouldn't be having this issue, but he won't have it.

'For the hundredth time, Ryan, I'm not moving in with you. You know how much grief we'll get. Your parents, my mum, my sister...'

'And, for the hundredth time, I don't care,' Ryan says, his voice rising. 'Can't you just forget about what people think for once?'

'Shh,' I hiss, looking around. 'Do you want to get us thrown out?'

Ryan looks down at Samantha again. She's wrapped her hand around her ventilator tube, so it looks like she's singing into a microphone. 'I just want to live in the same home as my daughter,' he mutters. 'I don't see why that's so unreasonable.'

When he puts it like that, nor do I.

I have visitors. By which I mean, Mum is crying quietly by my bedside and Amelia is staring daggers at me.

'What?'

'Look what you've done to Mum!'

I'm not sure I can take this right now. 'I haven't done anything to Mum. I know this isn't exactly fun for her, but it's not my fault.'

'Come on, Jessica,' Amelia says, like I'm an idiot. 'You must have done something wrong. Babies don't just fall out, three months early.'

I stare at her, stomach churning. 'Yes, they *do*. The

nurse said. There's a whole range of things that can cause premature labour and most of them are totally outside the mother's control. Did you know one third of premature births are unexplained? I didn't do anything wrong. I was just unlucky. This isn't my fault.'

What if it is? What if I did do something wrong? What if she dies because of me? I know something in unpasteurised milk can cause preterm labour. Do they pasteurise the stuff they put in chocolate?

'Jessica,' Amelia says sadly, 'you really need to face this. If you don't know what you did wrong this time, how are you supposed to stop it happening again?'

'Strangely enough, future children are not at the forefront of my mind right now.'

Six months of pregnancy still fresh in my mind, my baby on a ventilator and my nether regions feeling like they may collapse at any moment and let my internal organs fall out, and she expects me to be thinking about future kids? I'm not even thinking about future sex.

'Well, maybe they should be. You really need to pull yourself together.'

One day. She gave me *one day* to recover from this.

'Mum,' I say, stroking her hair, 'it's going to be okay. The doctors are wonderful here. They said she's a good weight and totally normal for her age. They do this all the time.'

Is it incredibly selfish to feel like they should be saying all this to me?

'Yes, of course,' Mum says, visibly pulling herself together and drying her eyes. 'She'll be absolutely fine. Why don't we talk about something more cheerful? Like your wedding. We could still put it together for the summer, you know, if we get working on it.'

I shift uncomfortably. 'I need to lose the baby weight first, Mum. And we'll be too busy looking after Samantha. Maybe next year.'

'Jessica!' Amelia hisses. 'How long are you going to put it off? You need to get married. Don't you know how embarrassing it's going to be for Mum, having you at home with a baby and no ring on your finger?'

'I've got a ring.'

'An *engagement* ring. It's not the same thing at all. And I don't know why you're planning a big white wedding, now you've got a baby. I can book the registry office, and you and Ryan can just pop down there and get the paperwork sorted.'

'Amelia, we're not talking about getting a TV licence. This is my *wedding*. I'm not popping from here to the registry office. Lots of people have babies before getting married these days. I bet most people won't bat an eyelid.'

'*Most people* aren't heavily involved in their local church. Mum's friends have *standards*.'

'Now, Amy,' Mum says. 'I think you'll find everyone's very understanding.'

Once, I called my sister Amy and she called me Jess. We were playmates. Friends. Not anymore.

'Or is Ryan the problem?' Amelia asks, with faux sympathy. 'Is he having second thoughts? I mean, you have rather let yourself go, haven't you? Perhaps I should talk to him.'

'No, thank you,' I say, clenching my fists to stop myself smacking her. 'Things are fine. I'll discuss it with him. Won't your car-parking be running out soon?'

Amelia checks her watch. 'Oh, yes. We'd better get

going, Mum.'

I have to forcibly restrain myself from kicking her out –
literally.

Chapter 2

When I next go and see Samantha, the ward round is going on and I can't get in. The doctors and nurses go round each baby in turn, discussing their progress. Only the parents of the baby they're discussing at the time are allowed in.

I retreat to the waiting room, which is occupied by a slightly chubby thirty-something woman with dark curly hair and the inevitable remains of a baby bump. She gives me a friendly and surprisingly genuine-looking smile as I enter.

'Hello new girl,' she says, in an unmistakably Welsh accent. 'I'm Gwen. Gwen Jones.'

'Jess Jackson.'

'Just had your baby yesterday?'

'The day before, actually, late on.'

'How old? What's her name?'

'I've named her Samantha. 26+4.'

'That's rough. 28 weeks my first one was, and that was bad enough.' She stretches out her legs. 'Is your partner here?'

I shake my head. 'Not today. I'm not sure if I'm sorry right now. Mostly, I want to beat him over the head with something.'

'Oh, that's completely normal. It'll wear off, you'll see.'

'Maybe.' I shift restlessly. 'What about you?'

'Gareth's home in Cardiff, looking after our older two.'

'Cardiff? How did you end up here?'

She rolls her eyes. 'We were up here on holiday when my water broke. I told the man it was a stupid idea, but after Carys was born at full term he was convinced it would be fine this time too. Now I'm stuck here until they have space in Cardiff. So I completely understand about wanting to hit your other half upside the head. Will you be staying in the flats?'

The hospital apparently has flats for NICU parents who aren't local. The nurses have already talked to me about them, since I don't actually need to be in the ward. I came out of labour without a graze, let alone a tear, although my nether regions are still feeling decidedly delicate. So I suppose Samantha's early arrival had one perk.

'I think so, when they discharge me. Until someone comes in who lives further away anyway. What are they like?'

'They're decent enough. Just round the corner, anyway. Helpful when you stumble down here to pump at 2am.'

'Yeah.' I watch her twirl a curl around her finger. 'What's your baby called?'

'Ianto.'

'What?'

'Yan-toe. Spelt I-A-N-T-O. It's Welsh.'

'Oh. Nice.'

A nurse comes to the door. 'Gwen, they're moving onto Ianto now.'

Gwen hauls herself to her feet. 'See you later then,' she says. 'Give me a knock when you get into the flats and I'll show you where everything is. I'm in number two.'

'Thanks,' I say, as she goes off with the nurse.

I sit for another minute. Then the door opens again, and someone else comes in.

This is a man. Tall, slim, dark ponytail and goatee, maybe mid 20s - like me. He's wearing blue jeans, a black T-shirt and Doc Martins and carrying a McDonalds bag. He's nothing like my type, and yet I surprise myself by finding him attractive. It must be the post-pregnancy hormones.

'Hello,' he says, flopping into a chair. 'I'm Ben. My baby's Edward. Born 8 days ago, 23 weeker. Yours?'

'Samantha. Yesterday. 26+4. I'm Jess,' I say, as he starts tearing into a hamburger. 'Is Edward's mother here?'

'No.'

'At work?'

'In Mauritius.'

'I'm sorry?'

'She's in Mauritius. On holiday. Sort of a babymoon, only the baby came first.'

'Oh.'

What sort of mother goes on holiday while her child is in the NICU?

I get out my hand cream, mostly for something to occupy myself.

Silence stretches out while he continues to destroy the hamburger.

'So, Edward,' I say. 'That's a nice name.'

He shrugs. 'It's all right. I like it better than her choice for a girl.'

'Which was?'

'Bella.'

I smirk. 'As in Twilight?'

He rolls his eyes. 'I stress the point: not my idea. She's a big fan.'

'How old is she, 17?' I try to joke.

'Close.'

'Oh.' I shift uncomfortably.

The door opens. It's the nurse again. She smiles at me. 'We're moving onto Samantha now.'

'Okay,' I say. 'Nice to meet you, Ben.'

'Likewise.'

And I exit hurriedly.

'How's she doing?' I ask the nurse as I approach Samantha's incubator, rubbing cream into my newly-scrubbed hands.

'Fine. We just put her milk up again.'

I sit by Samantha's incubator, perched on a stool, and stare at the red, shiny thing that's supposedly my baby.

I'm sure I should want to be by her side, but I don't even believe she's mine. She's a far cry from the babies on the TV. Mind you, from what I hear, most babies are.

'You should try talking to her,' the nurse says. 'She knows your voice from being in the womb. It's soothing for her.'

'Okay,' I say, but say nothing. I feel too awkward. There are people all around. And what do I say?

'I'll just pop out and give you some privacy.'

'Thanks.'

She leaves, and I stare at Samantha. Privacy is a relative term. I'm hardly alone with her.

I'm going to have to say something.

'So,' I say, 'the nurse says you like to hear me talk, so

here goes.'

I clear my throat. 'This was supposed to be easy, you know. I thought I'd be cooing away over you. But we're not supposed to be able to see each other yet. Well, you can't see me now because your eyes are still shut. It's probably just as well. I'm still all bloated, and my skin is terrible. You're not looking so good yourself, but that's not your fault.'

I pause to swallow the lump in my throat.

'I'm sorry,' I tell her. 'I don't know why this happened. I don't know if this is my fault. I *do* know I didn't do it deliberately. I know I complained a lot about being pregnant. I bet you'd be the same if you felt sick and exhausted all day, every day, for six months. Being pregnant sucks. But I hope you didn't think that meant I didn't want you. Because I did. I've always wanted you. It was just that growing you was a whole lot harder than I expected. When I said I wanted it to be over, I just meant I wanted to sleep through the rest of the pregnancy, or something. I didn't want to push you out before you were ready. This isn't how I wanted your life to start.'

She's crying. So much for being comforted by my voice. Her little face has gone redder and more screwed up than usual, and she's flinging out her limbs. But she can't make a sound. Because there's a tube down her throat. If you're not right beside her, you wouldn't know. And most of the time, there isn't anyone. So she cries alone.

And even if you are there, what can you do? Her immature skin is too sensitive to handle much contact. The most I can do is touch her hand or use the containment hold - basically putting my hands round her without quite touching. It doesn't feel like much. It's probably a blessing that she's asleep or drugged up most of the time. But no one who's less than a week old should be on morphine.

No one's life should start like this.

'Bye, baby,' I choke out and run away from my new reality.

Chapter 3

The next day, I meet Mum in reception and take her through to the NICU. This is the first time that we're visiting Samantha together. Mum is looking much calmer than last time she was in. She seems to have recovered her natural serenity.

Mum looks nothing like me. I'm blonde; she's a brunette. She's shorter and heavier, although she's lost a lot of weight in the last six months. She's actually very pretty, with dark brown eyes and lovely skin. My eyes are blue and too large, so I always look anxious. I take after my dad, though thankfully not in terms of the amount of body hair.

'How's she doing today?'

'Okay. No change, I think.'

I still don't feel I have a handle on what's going on. I'm not even sure I want to. Just let me live in ignorance. I don't need to know what the doctors are doing. The only questions I want to ask are the ones I know they can't answer, like 'Will she come home?' and 'Will she be healthy?'

'And how are you?'

'Okay.'

You know, the crazy thing is I feel good. Cheerful. Not even that tired. It makes no sense.

Maybe it's just not feeling sick for the first time in five months. So much for morning sickness being in the first trimester. It was all day, and all the way through. And I loathe feeling sick. And throwing up. Mind you, I didn't have it nearly as bad as some people. I was reading this blog by someone who'd had this nasty condition called hyperemesis gravidarum, which now features prominently in my vision of hell. It basically meant that she threw up ten or more times a day, every day. At one point, she ended up in hospital on a drip because she couldn't even keep down water and she was badly dehydrated. I don't know how she survived it. Certainly no one told me about *that* pre-pregnancy. If they had, I think I'd have got myself sterilised.

'Really?' Mum sounds sceptical.

I flash a smile. 'Yeah. I expect I'll crash soon, but for now I'm okay.'

We go through the first door into Neonatal. Here there are lockers, coat racks, a bin for rubbish and a sink. We have to leave our outer things - we wouldn't want them in the NICU anyway, it's far too hot - and bags. Then we have to roll up our sleeves to above the elbow, ditch all rings, bracelets and watches, wash our hands thoroughly and then apply alcohol hand gel. By the sink is a sign reminding us not to go in if we've been ill in the last forty-eight hours.

What do I do when that happens? What are the chances of me getting through the next however long without getting sick?

From this area, there are two doors. One is labelled 'NICU and High Dependency' and the other 'Special Care'. These are steps 1, 2 and 3 on the road to getting out of here. I can't help staring at the 'Special Care' door and wondering when - or if - Samantha will be moved through there. The two wards connect, but only the staff and babies are allowed through the connecting corridor. Us parents have to start here and be separated.

We go through the NICU door and down the corridor. On the left is the waiting room and further down on the right is apparently a pumping room. I hope it's going to be a bit more comfortable than the milking sheds used for cows.

We walk down the corridor, turn left at the main desk, enter the NICU and go straight to the sink.

'She looks good,' Mum says, quite untruthfully, when we finally make it to her incubator.

I look away, pretending to be interested in the monitors. The ventilator one shows green peaks when she breathes, and red ones when the ventilator does it for her. There's an awful lot of those.

Mum perches on a stool by the incubator, and starts talking to Samantha calmly, telling her the story of Noah's Ark. I envy her. Mum is the best advertisement for Christianity that I have ever met. She has a kind of inner peace and faith that allows her to accept that the worst in life is ultimately for the best, even if she doesn't understand why. She did everything she could to pass that on to us, but it just hasn't worked. We go to church and call ourselves Christians, but we're not. Not in the true sense, the one that Jesus would recognise.

I wish I could leave her here with Samantha. She's obviously far more comfortable with her than I am. But I can't. Rules are rules: a parent must accompany all visitors. And Ryan isn't here. Still. All I can say, he'd better be here to escort his mother. I will literally hide in the toilets if she comes on her own.

'Shall I bring in one of her blankets to put over her incubator?' Mum asks, when she finishes the story. 'I see some of the others have them.'

'It's to block some of the light from their eyes,' I explain, glancing around. 'And her eyes aren't open yet.'

'Still, it would personalise her space a bit. A lovely one arrived from Aunt Mildred this morning. A real proper handmade quilt, and I know you said you're not supposed to use them for babies now, so it'll just go to waste otherwise. And maybe a teddy for her cot. If that's allowed.'

'Sure,' I say, pretending to look at Samantha's food supply. 'Bring them in.'

At the moment, a machine feeds Samantha. It holds an oral syringe, connected to a tube that goes into her nose and down to her stomach. The machine pushes the milk through the tube at the unbelievably slow rate of 0.1ml an hour, which obviously no human could manage. She's never hungry, so she doesn't waste energy crying - ineffectually - for food. She needs those calories. Breathing, maintaining her temperature, digesting food and moving against gravity are hard work when your body isn't yet equipped for it.

'Are you going to do her cares while you're here?' the nurse asks, coming over.

"Cares" means changing her nappy - no easy task considering you have to put your hands through the incubator portholes - and wiping her down with cotton wool and sterile water. Her mouth is also cleaned, using a sponge on a stick that looks like a drumstick lolly.

Samantha doesn't like them much. As I wipe her, her tiny hands try to push me away. I'm amazed at the strength in her. They said she had good muscle tone for her gestation. At least she's ahead on one thing.

It surprises me that I don't mind cleaning up poo. I thought it would take me ages to get used to it, but I care more about her being comfortable. Hopefully that means the maternal instincts are starting to kick in. Although, I have to say, when I read that baby poo was yellow I was expecting more straw than highlighter pen.

I feel completely wiped out. I hadn't realised quite how out of shape I'd become. For most of the pregnancy, I just collapsed onto the sofa when I got home from work. Then the last few days I was pretty much on bed rest in hospital. Just existing feels exhausting.

I'm going to have to cram in some exercise, though goodness knows when.

Okay, I can do this.

The nurses say it's time to move from hand expression to the breast pump. I have my doubts. There doesn't seem to be much coming out.

I'm sitting in the pumping room. The front of it holds the essential tools for the pumping mum: a sink for yet more hand washing, a microwave for sterilising and multiple tubs full of bottles and oral syringes for the milk. I'm still on the 1ml syringes. The 100ml bottles look wholly unachievable.

The back of the room is divided into three cubicles by way of hospital curtains. Each has a padded plastic-covered chair, a footstool, a big yellow pump on a wheeled stand and a table covered in classic literature, such as *Heat* and *Grazia*.

I hold in my hands a pair of funnel-and-bottle contraptions. They bear a striking resemblance to a couple of air horns. If they make a similar noise, I may have to call the whole thing off.

As the nurse patiently explained, I put one onto my left boob, taking several attempts to get my nipple in the middle of the tube. Then I turn the machine on and hastily attempt the same with the right breast. After a couple of tries, the mini vacuum cleaner is sucking happily away. Theoretically, milk will now drip into the bottles.

Well, now what do I do? I can't read the aforementioned classic literature, due to having my hands full. Do I really have to sit for 20 minutes with my hands clamped to my chest like my bikini top has fallen off?

I suppose I do.

The news finishes on the radio and a song starts. 'All by Myself' by Celine Dion. Wonderful. Tears threaten to fall.

Noise as someone comes in. Even though they can't see me, I hastily try to blink the tears away.

'Who's in the shed?' calls Gwen's cheerful voice.

'Jess.'

'How are you getting on?'

I look down at myself. Top shoved up, bra hanging around my waist, middle getting cold, stretch marks on display, nipples being sucked worryingly far into the tube. 'Okay.'

'Cassandra, meet Jess. She's new.'

'Hi, Cassandra.'

Am I the only one who thinks introductions through a curtain are a bit weird?

'Hello, Jess,' Cassandra says, in a tone that suggests I'm

not. 'I brought my tweezers, Gwen. So I can do your eyebrows if you want.'

'Definitely. Let's get hooked up, and then I'm all yours.'

'How can you do that while you're on this thing?' I ask.

'Hands free pumping bra,' Gwen replies. 'Vital for sanity. They should really provide them on the NHS.'

There's movement in the cubicle next to me, and Gwen pulls back the curtain that separates us. 'There we go,' she says. 'Much more friendly.'

I flush and try to turn myself away.

'You've got nothing I haven't, chick,' Gwen says, looking amused. 'And, trust me, whatever modesty you've got left will soon be a thing of the past. Just wait until you've chatted with the doctor with your tits out.'

I tense. 'They don't come in here, do they?'

'Not here, no,' Gwen says, and I can't help but watch as she feeds her pump flanges into this odd bustier thing with practised ease. 'But when my first was in Special Care they didn't have a room like this, so I used to pump at her bedside and the doctors and nurses would just come and go. I guess once you've seen enough women on the pump you don't even think about it. It's like when I used to work at Boots and after a while I'd sell piles cream and vibrators without even blinking and wonder why the customers were embarrassed.'

'Where do I get one of those tops?'

'They sell them on Amazon,' Cassandra says, bringing her pumping kit into Gwen's space, along with the pump from the third cubicle. She turns out to be your quintessential yummy mummy. Tall, blonde, with long, perfectly-styled hair, flawless makeup and clothes that look like they were made for her. Just the barest hint of a mummy tummy. In other words, exactly the kind of woman I've spent the last six months desperate to smack.

I really have to take off my pyjamas and actually get dressed.

'But you can also cut holes in a basic sports top. Or even just a stretchy bra. There's a Tesco superstore not far away where you can get one. And, seriously, you need to. Apparently, you can get carpal tunnel syndrome from holding the bottles in place.'

Gwen grimaces. 'And that is not fun. I had that while I was pregnant with Carys.'

I'm finding this conversation increasingly surreal. Here are three women sitting around with their tits out, and one is plucking another's eyebrows.

'You'll get used to it,' Gwen says sympathetically, evidently seeing my expression. 'Welcome to your new life.'

I don't want a new life. I was quite happy with my old one.

Later that day, I collect my key and venture into my new accommodation. My home is about 40 miles from the hospital, but this is the nearest one with a NICU. I'm grateful I can stay here and don't have to commute in every day. I would hate to be so far away from Samantha.

It turns out that "flats" is a bit of a misnomer. I find myself in a short corridor bending round to the right with several doors off it. The one to my left is open, revealing a common room, with a sofa, table and chairs, and a TV. The next four doors are numbered. On the right is an opening leading to a kitchenette with a sink, a microwave, a fridge, a kettle and a few cupboards. The door at the end of the corridor has a sign on it indicating a shower room.

In room three - my new home - I find a single bed, a wardrobe, a chair and a nightstand with a lamp on it. Hardly a 5 star hotel, but it looks clean. It reminds me of the student flats Ryan stayed in for his 3rd year at university.

Slowly, I unpack my things. I check the view out of the window, but all I can see is another block of the hospital. At least there are a few plants growing outside, and I can see the sky.

I wander out of my room to look around better and turn as someone comes out of the shower room. It's the man from the waiting room. Ben. Slightly damp, and wearing a towel. *Just* a towel. I try not to gape. I fail.

He's not a hunk, exactly. He's... wiry, I think you call it. But there are certainly muscles there. And a light dusting of hair. And there's just something about him that makes me feel...

I hastily pull my gaze back up to his face. 'Um... hi.'
'Hey.'

'You're um... you're living here too?'

'Yup,' he says, rubbing his hair with a smaller towel. 'Fathers don't usually get in, but they had space and I managed to get them to make an exception, since Edward's mum isn't here. Could be kicked out any day, though, if someone else needs the room.'

I feel my gaze drifting downwards again and retrieve it. 'Oh dear,' I say weakly.

'But, while I'm here, let me know if there's anything I can do to help. I'm on leave from work so I can be here for Edward, and obviously I don't need to pump.' He laughs and rubs his nipples slightly. I catch my breath. 'I wouldn't get a lot out of these!'

'Uh...'

He grins at me. 'I'd better get dressed,' he says. He leans over and opens the door of the room next to mine. 'I'm in here. Feel free to knock any time.'

'Yeah.'

After he's gone in, I stand there for a minute, staring at his door. Then I give myself a shake.

What in the world am I doing? I gave birth less than a week ago and now I've got a crush.

I pull myself together and go to investigate the shower. In no way imagining what he looks like naked.

Chapter 4

When I get back from pumping again, it's lunch time and I'm hungry. This is my first meal in days not provided by the hospital, the café is closed and I'm going to have to venture out in search of food. Trouble is, I don't have a clue where to find it. I should have asked one of the nurses.

When I open the door that leads to the flats, I immediately hear voices in the common room, including Gwen's. I suppress the desire to hide in my room and eat biscuits, and go in.

'Honestly, I'd like to kill my mother-in-law,' Gwen complains, throwing her mobile phone onto the sofa. 'She's giving me hell about Ianto being born in England. Like it was *my* idea to go out of the country at seven months pregnant. If her son hadn't wanted to go to that bloody medieval reenactment thing, I would have given birth in Cardiff like I was supposed to. But no, it must be *my* fault that her grandson is an Englishman. Apparently, she thinks I heard some sort of siren call telling me to go to the north of England to have him. Despite the fact that I've lived in Wales for fifteen years, and I was born in Devon.'

'Bit of a nationalist, is she?' Cassandra asks, looking up from a baby manual.

'Understatement. I wouldn't mind, but Gareth told me that her grandfather's from Scotland! So she's not even pure blood herself. But you wouldn't think it to hear her talk.'

She spots me and gives me a grin. 'Hi, Jess. Don't mind me. Monster-in-law troubles. Have you moved in?'

'Just about. All I did was unpack, and then I had to pump again.'

'Bloody nightmare, isn't it? That thing rules your life. Have you had lunch?'

'Not yet. I was going to ask you where to find food.'

'Come with us. We're going on an exciting outing to Tesco.'

I've been in hospital - minus the ambulance ride from my local one - for six days when I finally step outside. The air feels weird and the cold makes me shiver. The sun is down, though it's not late. I'd almost forgotten it was winter.

I walk down the road with Gwen and Cassandra, feeling like I'm dreaming. It seems to take forever just to pass the hospital grounds. Then we reach some houses and finally a small row of shops, including a mini-market.

I select myself some microwave meals - all the flats' kitchen caters for - and some other essentials.

It seems incredible that other people are just going about their lives as normal. I guess when your life changes, you feel like everyone else's should change too, but they don't. The rest of the world just carries on, neither knowing nor caring that your part of it has come crashing down.

'Hey,' says a voice, when we step outside again.

I look up. It's Ben, leaning against a motorbike.

'Fancy a ride?'

I open my mouth to say no. Mum always said motorcycles were too dangerous.

'I've got a spare helmet.'

'Go on, Jess,' Cassandra says. 'Ben's a good driver and you need time away from the hospital.'

'I'll take your shopping back,' Gwen says. 'Go get a bit of air.'

'Thanks,' I say gratefully.

So I'm flying round the streets after dark, on the back of a motorbike. My arms are around Ben, who is solid and warm, and I feel a spark of excitement I haven't felt in a long time, though whether it's from him or the bike ride I don't know.

And, for the first time, I feel like I don't want to wake up from this dream.

'That was wonderful,' I tell him, when we get back to the hospital. 'Thanks very much.'

'No problem. I always find a bike ride helps clear the head. I'll take you anytime.'

I hear a double meaning in those words, mentally chastise myself and retreat to the safety of my room as soon as I can.

Yet another pumping session down, and Cassandra's done a lovely job on my eyebrows. I sleepwalk to the milk fridge by the NICU door to put in my latest pathetic offering and meet today's nurse. 'Oh good, I was just coming to get more for Samantha,' she says.

I check the fridge and am alarmed to see that there's nothing in my little cardboard tray. I hand over the new syringe. 'How long is that going to last?'

'About two hours. How often are you pumping?'

'Every two hours.'

'Night time too?'

'Yes.'

'Oh well,' she says. 'You're still keeping up. Sometimes the milk is slow to come in. Just keep at it, and before you know it you'll be over-producing. You are making sure to eat and drink enough and get plenty of rest, aren't you?'

Is there a new mother anywhere who gets plenty of rest?

'Yeah.'

'Have you tried looking at photos of Samantha while you're pumping?'

That just makes me cry.

'Or doing relaxation exercises? You can try visualising streams and waterfalls.'

'Right,' I say quickly. 'I can do that. I'll work something out.'

What am I supposed to do if I can't make enough milk for her?

'And don't worry about it,' the nurse adds cheerfully, as she heads back into the NICU. 'That's the worst thing you can do.'

Wonderful. That's a big help.

'God, they always say that, don't they?' Gwen says, as I relate the conversation in the common room. 'You can't make enough milk, but don't worry. You can't conceive for two years, but don't worry. Your left leg is hanging by a thread, but don't worry...'

'But what if I really can't make enough milk?' I ask

quietly.

'It's only been a week,' Cassandra says. 'And there's lots of things you can try to get things going.'

'The nurse said something about visualising streams.'

Gwen grimaces. 'I wouldn't recommend that, personally. I tried listening to this CD of water sounds, but it just meant I spent every pumping session desperate to pee. But you can try...'

She starts reeling off a whole list of things. I rummage in my pumping bag for a pen and paper and have her start again so I can write them down. I'll have to call Ryan and get him to go to Tesco.

'I've got a good book on breastfeeding that I'll lend you,' Cassandra says. 'So really, don't worry. Your left leg is still firmly attached.'

I manage a small smile.

Don't worry. Right.

I'm just getting my trainers on when I get a text from Ryan telling me he's here.

'I'm just heading out for a walk,' I say, when we meet in reception.

He gives me a hug. 'I'll come with you.'

'I'm going to try and have a walk every day,' I explain, as we get out of the hospital. 'To get some fitness back. I can hardly find the energy to stand for Samantha's cares.'

'Oh good,' Ryan says. 'The fresh air will help. And the exercise will help you get your figure back.'

I grab his arm, stopping us both. 'Get my figure back?' I repeat. 'Ryan, I gave birth *one week ago,* and you're talking about me *getting my figure back?*'

He looks like I've pulled a gun on him. 'I just meant...

Jess, you're the one who's spent the last few months moaning about how much you hate being fat.'

'I'm fat, am I?' I ask, fists clenching by my sides.

'No!' he says quickly. 'I didn't mean *I* think you're fat, just... you know... I... Can we just forget I said anything?'

'No!' I snap back. 'You obviously do. Even though all the weight gain is *your fault* because *you* got me pregnant.'

I start walking again, as fast as I can manage. Ryan strides along beside me. 'Why is it just *my* fault? You were there too, you know.'

'Because you were the one who thought it would be okay to stop using condoms and just rely on the pill, and it clearly wasn't!'

'Well, you agreed.'

'That's not the point!'

'Fine,' Ryan says. 'How about we just stop talking about this?'

I don't look at him. 'Okay,' I mutter.

I see him shake his head out of the corner of my eye. 'Oh man, I can't wait until your hormones settle down and we can have a sensible conversation again.'

I stop us again. 'Excuse me?'

He crosses his arms. 'Well, it's impossible to talk to you at the moment. Your mood changes in seconds, you take everything the wrong way, you're so grumpy all the time.'

I can't believe I'm even having this conversation.

'My baby's in the hospital on life support and you think I'm *too grumpy*?'

'I know she's in the hospital, just...' Ryan fiddles with his watch. '... can't you put it aside once in a while and just be with me?'

I take a step away from him. 'No, I can't. And I can't believe you can.'

Ryan holds up his hands in surrender. 'Fine, you can't do it. Well, forgive me if I don't much feel like coming around just to be yelled at.'

'Fine!'

'Enjoy your walk. I'm going back home.'

'Go!' I yell after him as he walks back the way we came. 'See if I care!'

When I get back from my walk, I'm drawn to the hospital shop and I'm sorely tempted to replace any calories I've burnt on my walk. You'd think a hospital shop would promote healthy eating, but it's stuffed to the ceiling with chocolate, crisps and fizzy drinks. This will not help with my weight loss efforts.

I could be good and just buy a magazine to cheer myself up.

'Hey, Jess,' Ben says cheerfully, coming in wearing running gear. I stare at him. I've never been into the fitness freak type, but somehow he makes sweaty look good. I feel a flutter inside, like a butterfly is loose in there.

'Hi.'

'Just been for a walk?'

'Yeah.' I must look sweaty too. And I bet my face is red. And my hair has given me a little halo of frizz. 'Working on getting rid of the baby weight.'

He grabs a bottle of Lucozade. 'Bit early for that, isn't it? Aren't you supposed to rest as much as possible for the first six weeks?'

'Well,' I say, blushing, 'I'm just trying to get back a little fitness. You need stamina in here.'

'That you do,' he says, paying for his drink. 'Just don't overdo it. And don't go fretting about a couple of extra pounds. You don't want to end up like one of those so-called supermodels with their bones sticking out. Personally, I think a real woman is a cuddly woman.'

He flashes me a smile and heads out.

I gaze after him. I think I'm falling in love.

Where did that thought come from?

'He's compartmentalising,' Gwen says, when I've finished complaining about Ryan later that day. 'Keeping the different parts of his life separate. Gareth does it too. It's flipping annoying at times, but it's normal. It doesn't mean he doesn't care.'

'Joseph too,' Cassandra says. 'I hate it. We had this big fight once, and I cried for hours while he went off to play golf with his mates like nothing had happened. I thought he'd stopped loving me. It nearly caused a divorce, until my mum explained it. I still have to keep reminding myself that it doesn't mean what I think it does.'

'Men!'

'Men!'

'Why do we bother with them?'

Sometimes I wonder.

Ryan and I went to high school together. One of his mates knocked me over by my locker, and he picked my books up. A day or two later, he was hanging awkwardly around there waiting to ask me out. He took me to the cinema and knocked a slushy down my dress. I'm still not sure why I agreed to a second date, but we've been together ever since.

Ryan is... a lad. He goes to work in overalls and steel-capped boots and changes into battered jeans and a football shirt when he gets home. He has a whole group of mates that he's known since school, who all have nicknames based on embarrassing things they did once, at least a decade ago. Together they get pissed, sing stupid songs, play football, and occasionally tie each other naked to stationary objects. He doesn't talk about feelings, "women's stuff" or anything during a football match.

He's tallish and stocky-ish, with the beginnings of a beer belly. He has sandy hair that he keeps really short, because it's curly and when he was a kid his mum made him have it long and everyone thought he was a girl. He has a broad face that is really only designed for a grin. He's not bad-looking, but you wouldn't find him advertising cologne.

I find myself picturing Ben. He seems different. Exciting. And there's precious little to get excited about in this place.

Ryan is waiting outside the flats when I emerge after my evening pumping.

'You came back.'

'Yeah.'

'I'm sorry about earlier,' I say, slightly grudgingly.

'Me too.'

'Are you going in to see her?'

He shifts uncomfortably. 'I did. I forgot to tell you earlier, I went to Tesco and got that stuff you wanted.'

'Thanks,' I say, and give his hand a squeeze.

He grins. 'Can I come in for coffee?'

I manage a weak smile. 'As long as that's not a

euphemism.'

We make our way round the corner, into the flats and to my room. No one else seems to be around.

'Can you give me a cuddle?' I ask, when we're safely inside.

We lie down on the bed together. It's odd to be lying on a single bed together again. We haven't done this since I visited him at uni.

Suddenly, I start to cry. For the first time since the day Samantha was born, I completely break down and howl. I just keep on and on while Ryan holds me, until my phone chimes to tell me it's time for me to go and help with Samantha's cares.

'Just stay here,' Ryan says, catching my arm as I start to get up. 'It's not like they can't do it without you. You're not in any fit state to go.'

'No, I have to,' I say, pushing him away. 'There's so little I can do for her, I have to do this.'

So I drag myself back to the NICU - trying and failing to stop crying - Ryan in tow. I start getting things ready - cotton wool, a warm dish of water and a clean nappy that would be too small for some of my cousin's dolls - but I can't stop crying.

Finally, one of the doctors takes me aside. 'I really think you should leave it,' he says kindly. 'You're obviously too upset to do this.'

'That's what I said,' Ryan chimes in. I suppress the urge to elbow him in the ribs.

I give up. I nod.

'And you know your baby picks up on your emotional state and you don't want to cause her stress, do you?'

Oh, wonderful. Now I'm a bad mother. Thanks a lot.

'Have you been googling her condition, by any chance?'

'Oh, she loves Google.'

'Because you know it's a bad idea. Every case is different. It'll only get you upset.'

So, now it's unreasonable of me to be upset that my baby can't breathe for herself.

'I told you so,' Ryan says, nudging me.

I want to smack him.

'I haven't been googling,' I mutter.

The doctor keeps talking, but I don't know what he's saying. I'm just standing there, still crying and thinking, 'Shut up, or I'm going to hit you.'

Finally, he does and I hurry out, Ryan following behind. I feel desperate and drained and terrified.

This isn't a dream.

Chapter 5

Dear everyone
Samantha is now one week old! So far, her issues have all been
routine for her gestation. She is still getting some IV fluids, but will
soon be entirely fed on mummy milk. Ventilator weaning is
progressing slowly. Her eyes are starting to open, and she can open her
left eye a little bit. We've discovered she has a light covering of blonde
hair. She has maintained her birth weight this week and the doctors
are pleased with her progress so far.

Thank you for all the messages, cards and presents.
Jess, Ryan and Samantha

I finish my Facebook update and add a picture of
Samantha's first nappy compared to a regular newborn
one. It's my best effort at helping people visualise how
small she is. I don't want to share pictures of her. I don't
want to scare people, and I'm afraid of their comments -
well meaning though I'm sure they'll be.

Despite my attempt at a cheery update, all is not well.
Now my bubble of denial has burst, I feel like I'm
constantly tense. Every time I walk into the NICU, I
expect to hear bad news. It doesn't help that I always
seem to be the last to know what's happening with
Samantha. Even when I think I'm up-to-date, things

change so fast around here that the next time I come in the plans seem totally altered. There's a shift change every 12 hours and a new nurse or doctor on each shift every two or three days. I recognise faces, but can't remember anyone's names. And they all seem to have their own ideas about her treatment. She's my daughter and yet I have almost no control over what happens to her. I don't feel like her mother. I don't even feel like me. I barely feel like a human being. And, every minute of every day, I am terribly afraid of what's to come.

I wake suddenly from a dream where I'm a zombie cow and find I've fallen asleep on the pump. It's a good thing it cuts off after 20 minutes on the preemie setting, or I dread to think what state my nipples would be in. I'd stop traffic walking around in a t-shirt if they didn't go back down.

I check the clock. It's time to pump again. Good thing breast milk keeps for a few hours at room temperature. I can't afford to throw any away.

I wonder if I should bed down in this room. Just disconnect from the pump every few sessions for cleaning and go right back on it. It would save time, and it feels like I live here anyway. I could be the pumping room hermit. Years from now, I could be a hospital legend.

But I can't just start the pump again. What if they've run out of milk while I've been asleep?

I haul myself out of the chair, wipe away the drool, bottle the milk and take it to the fridge. As I feared, the nurse is standing there.

'Just in time!' she says cheerfully, and I suppress the urge to smack her.

I trudge back and hook up again.

I need to sleep. I haven't slept for much more than an hour at a time in days. I've given up wearing my contacts, because my eyes are so sore. I keep bumping into things. I stop talking halfway through sentences because I've forgotten what I was going to say. I feel like I'm walking through soup.

Gwen comes in, yawning. 'Morning,' she says. 'You look like death warmed up.'

'Fell asleep at the pump.' Even talking feels like too much effort.

She frowns. 'That's a new one on me. How often are you pumping at night?'

'Every two hours.'

'Flipping hell, Jess, you can't keep that up round the clock! Not unless you want to go crackers. Much more and you'll find yourself at the supermarket in your dressing gown, screaming at the cabbages. Trust me, I've done it. Nearly got myself sectioned.'

'It's not like I'm doing this for fun,' I snap. 'I'm just not making enough milk. I can't leave it any longer, or they'll run out. I don't need you rubbing my failure in my face.'

'Look,' Gwen sighs, taking my hand, 'your breasts were designed to make milk for a baby, not a pump. Some women's accept the substitute, and some just don't.'

'So, you're saying there's nothing I can do?'

'No, I'm saying that if the pump doesn't work for you it's not your fault. The chances are that you're making plenty of milk, but the pump isn't getting it out. And, even if you weren't, it's still not your fault. There are still plenty of things to try.'

'But what am I supposed to do right now?' I ask,

clutching at my hair. 'I'm barely keeping up. Any minute she's going to overtake me, and they'll have to give her formula. And I was reading that book Cassandra has about all the health problems and why premature babies need their mother's milk more than ever and...'

'That would be why I told you not to read it,' Gwen interrupts. 'The last thing you need is a guilt trip. We'll work on it. And, as a temporary measure... why don't you take some of mine?'

'What?'

'Seriously. My boobs love the pump. I could feed three easily. Any dairy farmers get wind of me and I'm in big trouble. And Ianto's only a few weeks older than Samantha, so my milk should be fine for her. Just use a clean syringe and take what you need from my bottles until you catch up.'

I stare at her and feel like crying. 'Really?'

'Course.' She grins. 'We NICU mums need to stick together.'

I grab her and pull her into a hug, sobbing on her shoulder.

'It'll be fine,' she says into my hair. 'There's always a way through. Just don't tell the nurses. How much do you want to bet there'll be a health and safety rule about it?'

Ryan has finally turned up to visit Samantha - by which I mean he's standing awkwardly by her incubator, looking everywhere but at her - when the nurse says casually, 'Have you held her yet?'

We look at each other. 'No.'

'Would you like to?'

I can't help thinking what a ridiculous question that is.

I think they forget what a big deal this is to us. Of course I want to hold her. I've been waiting a week with a dull pulling sensation in my chest, as my natural mothering instincts had to be suppressed. And I need it to start off the bonding process.

It's not a case of just picking her up. I have to get settled in a chair by the incubator. The nurse arranges a blanket over my arm and shoulder, and gets out a roll of tape to fix the ventilator tubes to my shoulder. The tubes have to be briefly disconnected to move them out of the incubator, which freaks me out. Then she is lifted and plopped into my arms and quickly wrapped up in the blanket.

I always expected that rush of love would overwhelm me the first time I held her. But then, I thought that it would be right after she was born. There would be a joyful cry of 'It's a girl!' (or a boy - we wanted a surprise. We certainly got it.) and I'd be handed this squalling creature, who I would instantly worship and do anything for. As it is, I feel nothing of the sort.

I'll never have that moment. That reward for enduring pregnancy and labour. I feel cheated.

I'm crying a little, and I don't really know why. Disappointment? Emotional exhaustion? Or is the rush of love just a myth and this is it?

She weighs nothing. "Less than a bag of sugar" people say cheerfully.

'Look out, because your tiny baby will soon feel really heavy!' the nurse says.

Yes, that's the part to focus on.

She's right, though.

When I next go to see Samantha, I experience a momentary panic to find her hooked up to a bag of blood.

'It's normal,' the nurse reassures me. 'We have to take blood from her several times a day to test her oxygen levels, but she can't make her own red blood cells yet, so we have to replace them.'

It's a disturbing thought really. Makes her sound like some kind of vampire. A *Blade*-type one anyway.

There's a standard hospital bag, but underneath it is a tiny pouch - which I guess is her serving. It's sort of cute.

The doctor comes over. 'Just to let you know we've done a scan of her heart.'

Mine instantly starts pounding.

'It looks fine,' the doctor reassures me. 'What it is, all babies have an extra tube in their hearts. In the womb, the heart works differently. The tube closes up when they're full term, but because Samantha was so early hers is still open. That's completely normal. Her heart is still working, just not at optimal production, so we want to try and close it.'

I have sudden visions of open-heart surgery and feel sick. 'How?'

'Ibuprofen.'

Huh?

'Ibuprofen?'

'Yes.'

'The stuff you take for aching muscles?'

'That's the one.' She smiles. 'I realise it sounds a bit odd, but it often works and it won't do her any harm or put her at risk, so we'll try that first. If we're lucky, the tube will close right up and the problem will be solved.'

'And if it doesn't?'

'With any luck, it should close on its own as she gets near her original due date. As long as it's not causing her significant issues, we'll just wait.'

'And if it does cause problems?'

'Well, we'll cross that bridge when we come to it.'

Has that phrase ever comforted anyone, ever?

Chapter 6

Samantha is now two weeks old. She's been practising opening her left eye in recent days and can manage to open it wider and for longer than she could before. No activity in the right eye that I've seen so far.

Now that her skin has matured, they are starting to bring down the humidity in her incubator. Once it gets down low enough, she will graduate to wearing clothes instead of just a nappy. Which means we will have to buy some, as I fear all the 0-3 months babygros I bought may be a tiny bit too big...

I'm beginning to think that those advocates of a strict routine may have a point. I'm getting far less sleep than I always thought I needed and yet it's actually easier to get out of bed - even in the middle of the night. Last night I woke up and felt like death, and I really thought it had finally caught up with me. It wasn't until I got to the pumping room and looked at the clock that I realised it was only an hour since my last session. Now I check my phone before I get up.

The 24 hour schedule also makes the time fly by. If I'd ever thought about what this would be like, I'd have expected every minute to feel like a day. Like it does when you're waiting for something exciting - or having a smear test. But between pumping, getting ready for pumping, cleaning up after pumping, sleeping, eating, visiting

Samantha and taking a walk and a shower, I don't have time to blink. Or think. And that can only be a good thing.

Ryan has an odd look on his face as we walk towards Neonatal together. 'What's that smell? It's kind of... sweet?'

'Fenugreek.'

His brow crinkles. 'What kind of Greek?'

I sigh. 'Fenugreek. It's a herb that's supposed to help with milk production. They also use it to flavour artificial maple syrup, so it makes you smell like that. You think this is bad; you should smell my pee.'

Ryan looks mildly revolted. 'No, thank you.'

I can't believe I said that. Gwen was right. Giving birth and multiple occurrences of getting my boobs out in front of strangers have destroyed my sense of modesty.

We both wash our hands, yet again. Mine are really starting to suffer. The skin on the back - which I have to admit I previously didn't always wash properly - is cracking. And I'm going to have to put on alcohol hand gel to touch Samantha. And that is going to hurt. I must ask Cassandra what her secret is.

I endure the pain so that I can hold her little hand. By which I mean, so she can wrap her little hand around my fingertip.

'Do you want to dress her?' the nurse asks, with a smile on her face.

I stare at her. 'Really?'

'Really. I've got a vest for her in the drawer.'

She gets it out. It's white with pink clouds on it and looks like it belongs on a doll. It is kind of cute, though.

'Why is it held together with Velcro?' Ryan asks.

'It's much easier to get on and off, and accommodates the wires better.'

I gingerly wrap her in the vest, and then stand back and admire her.

It's amazing how much difference clothes make. It's just a silly little vest, but it seems like a massive step towards her being a real baby. I mean, I *know* she's a real baby, but, quite honestly, she still looks more like an alien. Though, at least, by this point I've more or less accepted that she's *my* alien.

I feel a surge of optimism that things may actually turn out okay.

'I think she's doing the YMCA.'

My friend Laura delivers her verdict of Samantha, after staring at her for a full minute. I have to laugh. Samantha does indeed have her skinny little arms above her head in what looks like a wonky M.

'Not too scary, then?'

'I googled images of premature babies before I came, so I knew what to expect.'

That's typical Laura. Of all my friends, she's the one I admire the most, for her maturity and good sense. Also, she has really shiny hair.

I look down at Samantha. 'You're the only one who's come, you know. Out of the girls. Mum comes several times a week - even Amelia comes sometimes - but no one else.'

Laura squeezes my hand. 'Don't take it personally. We looked at the photos together. Martha instantly decided she had to make a pot of tea, Claire burst into tears, Carol wouldn't look at them at all and Daisy said... well, you know she has that short circuit between her brain and her mouth. We all felt you'd be better off if she didn't come.'

I have to concede that point.

'Even Ryan is only coming up twice a week.'

'Apparently, the depot is manic at the moment, with the new year DIY rush.'

'I suppose.' I toe the floor. 'It probably doesn't help that I keep yelling at him.'

'I'm sure he understands you're under a lot of stress. You've been together for years and you've always been happy. Besides, women are better at this sort of thing. I'm only sorry I couldn't get in before now.'

'How's work?'

Laura is a fund-raising manager, currently working for a cancer charity I can't remember the name of. She started going door-to-door at university and amazingly wasn't put off.

'Oh, it's going well. Although, I've been thinking of changing jobs. I think it's time for a new cause. Bliss is advertising.'

Bliss is a charity for premature babies. I feel warm inside.

'Really?'

'Really.' She smiles at me. 'I've never really thought about it before, but I've been doing some research. There's been some major advances in the last 50 years or so, but we're getting to the point where the current technology isn't enough. I think the future is in developing artificial wombs to transfer the babies into. That way we could really push back the limits on when premature babies could survive from. Maybe one day we could even do an entire pregnancy like that.'

'That's a fantastic idea.'

I would *love* to skip the pregnancy and just get the baby at the end. Partly because it was a pretty miserable experience, but mostly because my future children might well be safer in a machine than in me.

I wish I knew why Samantha was born early. It was probably an infection, or something like that, but I can't help but worry that I'm defective. Couldn't carry my baby to term, can't make milk. What does that make me if not a failure as a woman?

'And I thought we could make that the cause for the fun run this summer.' Laura's voice pulls me out of my thoughts. 'But you're excused this year.'

'No!' I surprise myself by saying. 'I can do it. I'll just put Samantha in the pram. Assuming... Well, you know.'

'Have they given you any reason to think she won't come home?'

'No.' I feel tears pricking my eyes. 'They say it's all routine so far. But she's so small and she was so early...'

It's incredible to think that a baby born three months early can be routine to anyone.

'Well, then. Just have to wait.'

Patience is not my greatest virtue.

Cassandra recommends slathering my hands in cream and putting gloves on, every time I pump. So I do. And it does help.

After what feels like my millionth pumping session, I stumble out of my cubicle. As I'm transferring my still-pathetic offering to a syringe, my tired fingers fumble and I drop the bottle onto the floor. I stare at the mess in disbelief.

And then I am - quite literally - crying over spilt milk.

'Any progress?' Gwen asks, coming in.

I just stand there and sob. Gwen takes in the situation. 'Oh, chick, don't cry. It'll be fine.'

She gives me a hug while I try to get myself together again.

'Any luck with the Fenugreek?'

'No. I'm up to the maximum dose now and still nothing.'

'Bugger. But there's an entire health food shop full of stuff that might work. Sometimes it takes a while to find the right one.'

I sigh. 'I was thinking of asking the doctor about the prescription drug. I just don't think I can keep going long enough to try everything else out. Though, I'll get Ryan to buy some Blessed Thistle. No harm in trying and it'll be a few days before I can get to the doctor.'

'It's also good for gas,' Gwen says. 'Not that you have it.'

I escort Amelia to inspect Samantha (I'm not sure it counts as a visit). She's getting some more blood, which Amelia finds distasteful. For once, I don't blame her.

Something has clicked in Samantha's mind, and she's now opening both eyes properly. Her eyes are slightly freaky. They don't really have any colour; they're just black discs. You know on fantasy TV shows where someone turns evil? Like that. It's a bit creepy. I hope that won't last long.

I'd never have chosen to have her so early, but it is kind of cool that I get to see this stage when most parents don't. And regular newborns just look huge to me now. It seems amazing that anyone could see them as fragile. Someone sent me a 'tiny baby' babygro, and I laughed. These manufacturers think 7.5lb constitutes a tiny baby? They have no clue.

'What is that they're putting in her milk?' Amelia asks, as the nurse fixes Samantha's next syringe.

'Fortifier powder. They add it to breast milk to give her some extra calories.'

'Your stuff isn't good enough, then?'

I resist the urge to smack her. 'All the babies get it. They use a lot of calories because they have to work so hard to breathe and everything.'

'I suppose that's what happens when you can't keep them in long enough.'

I hate visiting time.

'Did they manage to fix her heart?'

'It's not broken. But no. They reckon the tube's narrowed a bit, but not closed. We'll have to wait and see if it rights itself when she gets near her due date.'

Eventually, Amelia has had enough. As I trail wearily out of the NICU, I see Gwen coming up from the pumping room and smile. Her attention, however, seems to be fixed beside me.

'Well, there's a blast from the past,' she says, approaching with a smile on her face. 'Amy, isn't it?'

I turn to Amelia. I think she's gone pale, though it's hard to tell under all that makeup.

'I think you're mixing me up with someone else,' Amelia says stiffly.

'Palma 2007? You were on your hen holiday, and your fluffy blonde friend got off with my mate Ken with the obscene tattoo.'

My eyes widen, and I turn to Amelia. 'Karen did that? Wasn't she married then?'

Amelia ignores me. 'Oh... yes,' she says, apparently with great reluctance. 'Gwen, wasn't it?'

'That's me. So, how have you been?'

'Very well. You?'

'Oh, not bad. Married with three kids now. What about you? Did you marry him in the end?'

'Yes, of course.'

'Really? Only you didn't seem sure.'

Amelia clenches her fists. Her knuckles go white. 'Just a few pre-wedding jitters. Completely normal. We're very happy.'

'Did you ever see... anyone... again?'

Is it me, or was she going to say a name?

'No.'

'Ah, well. What happens on holiday stays on holiday, right?'

'If you say so,' Amelia says. She checks her watch. 'I really must be going. Nice to see you again, Gwen.'

'Pleasure's all mine.'

Amelia hurries off down the corridor, with barely a glance at me. I stare after her.

'So, how do you know Amy?' Gwen asks.

'She's my sister.'

'Really? I didn't notice any resemblance between you.'

'No, there isn't much. But anyway, what was that about?'

'Just what you heard,' Gwen says, as we start to walk towards the flats.

'Yeah, but... there's more to it than that, isn't there?

Pre-wedding jitters? Please tell me she did something I can blackmail her with?'

Gwen grins at me. 'You don't like her very much, do you?'

I pull a face. 'I try to, but she's such a snooty bitch.'

Gwen laughs. 'Yeah. She's nicer pissed, though.'

'Come on,' I wheedle. 'You know something, and I need to know it too. She's giving me hell over having Samantha before getting married - and early - and I have to get something on her.'

'Oh, I don't know. Altering the balance of power like that...'

'Please. *Please*.'

'I'm not telling you,' Gwen says, ably resisting my best begging face. 'But she doesn't need to know that. You tell her that I'll spill the beans if she doesn't leave you alone. Fair enough?'

'Okay,' I agree reluctantly. 'But it's good, right? It's enough to get her to lay off?'

'I think it'll do the trick,' Gwen says. 'And, if necessary, I can provide photographic proof.'

Wonderful.

Chapter 7

Samantha is now three weeks old and weighed in at between 2lb 9oz and 2lb 10oz on Wednesday. The verdict from those who don't see her every day is that she has grown.

Ventilator weaning continues slowly. Although she doesn't like it much, Samantha seems reluctant to lose its support just yet. Hopefully in a few weeks, when her lungs are bigger, she will be able to come off it.

'We're going to try her on CPAP,' the nurse tells me when I go in to see Samantha.

I look blankly at her. I don't know if it's strange, but I just can't make myself read ahead about her care. I have this mad superstition that it'll jinx her progress.

'It's the next stage up from the ventilator. It doesn't breathe for her, but it helps her. Basically, it blows down her nose all the time and helps her inflate her lungs. It's like with blowing up a balloon. Getting it started is the hard part and after that it's easy.'

'Okay,' I nod, feeling somewhat dazed.

'Her tube needs changing anyway,' the nurse says kindly. 'We'll have a new one on standby and if it looks like she's not coping we'll get her back on the ventilator straight away. But the doctors think she can manage.'

'But... she doesn't always breathe on her own,' I say,

tension gripping my insides. 'The monitor keeps showing missing breaths. There's one now.'

She nods. 'It's actually quite hard to breathe normally with the tube in. And some babies start using it as a crutch. Once it's out, she should pick up every breath herself. And if she doesn't, we'll act. Yes?'

I nod, but it's not really okay. It should be a wonderful thing that she's moving on, but it's too scary. Right now, I know the ventilator is getting oxygen into her. Rationally, I know that she's monitored all the time and the doctors won't let her stop breathing, but it's still hard to believe that my tiny baby can manage on her own. I never thought the letting go would start before I really had her.

'Microwave's stopped working again,' Ben says, coming into the common room holding a plastic dish of something. 'Are you interested in half a lukewarm lasagne?'

'Tempting as it is, I have a lovely pasta salad here that's served cold, so I'll stick with that.'

He flops down next to me on the sofa. 'What are you watching?'

'*Glee*.'

He pulls a face. 'Nothing better on?'

'I like *Glee*. The early stuff anyway.'

He sighs. 'All right, then. *Glee* it is. At least it's not a soap.'

We sit together. Slowly, we shift closer together. Our knees touch, then our hips. Ben lays an arm over the sofa back, which migrates to my shoulders. I let my head fall onto his shoulder.

I laugh at something, and he turns to look at me. I

look up at him. His lips are so close...

My phone alarm goes off to tell me it's time to pump again, and I jump. 'Sorry, I have to go,' I say quickly, scrambling to my feet. 'Nose to the grindstone. Or breast. Or something. Anyway, see you later.'

And I run away.

I'm still not sure what this is. I've been attracted to other guys from time to time, but this is more. Is it hormones going mad? Or that I have more opportunity to get close to Ben than my other crushes? Or because I feel so far away from Ryan right now, physically and emotionally?

Could it be a sign that Ryan isn't the one I'm meant to be with?

Samantha lasts two hours on CPAP and then seems to run out of energy and goes back on the ventilator. The nurses make a point of telling me that this is not a step backwards, but a sign that she's nearly ready. I nod a lot and try to pretend I'm not relieved.

Back in my room, thinking of Ryan, out of nowhere I feel a stab of mad resentment. Because, in the last year, *everything* has changed for me, almost beyond recognition. And for him... nothing. He comes to see me at the hospital - when he can be bothered - instead of me coming over, and pops in to see Samantha while he's here. Big deal. It just isn't fair.

I'm suddenly angry. Furiously angry. Incandescent with rage. Forget wanting to smack someone, I want to destroy something. Smash it to pieces.

I can't remember ever feeling like this before. I don't know what to do with it. I try to beat a pillow, but it doesn't help. I want to smash my fist through the wall, but I can't afford to get thrown out of here.

I pace up and down in my room, clenching my fists, nails digging so deep into my palms I think they may leave permanent dents, not knowing what to do.

By the time Ryan calls, I'm starting to come out of it. His voice, however, brings another wave. I try to control it.

'Are you coming up tonight?'

'No, I'm going out to the pub with the lads.'

'Oh, wonderful,' I snap. 'You're leaving me here on my own and going out with your mates.'

'Yes, I am,' Ryan snaps back. 'You know why, Jess? I'm celebrating my birthday. Which was yesterday, in case you're interested.'

'Oh.'

I feel a sharp stab of guilt. I forgot his birthday. And I mean *completely* forgot. Haven't even thought about it.

'Well, did you really think it would be the same as last year?' I say, covering my guilt with anger.

Last year I planned a full-on surprise party for him. It took months to set up. I invited all the friends who'd moved away, bought industrial quantities of booze and hired the village hall. He got completely plastered, snogged his old science teacher - which I generously didn't mention again - and ended up doing a rather wobbly strip tease on top of a table. The lads of the village still talk about that night. So do the girls, though not for the same reasons.

'No, I didn't think it would be like last year,' he says. 'I wasn't expecting a big do. I don't mind not getting a present, or even a card. But you went the whole day and didn't even manage a "Happy Birthday". I really didn't think *that* was too much to ask.'

He hangs up.

And I start to cry.

I bring my dinner - microwave cottage pie in case you're interested - into the common room, where Gwen is eating something unidentifiable and watching TV. She's watching a show I've never seen before, that seems to involve a lot of sex scenes. Including one with two women kissing, which has me clearing my throat and looking away.

'Do you mind if I turn over?'

'Yes!' Gwen says quickly, though not angrily. 'This is my favourite show. And this is the closest I'll ever get to kissing her.'

'Oh!' I shift awkwardly. 'So you're... um... er...?'

'Bisexual.'

'Oh. Well... that's okay.'

Gwen looks vaguely amused. 'I'm so glad you think so,' she says, with a touch of sarcasm.

There's a silence. To me, it's horribly awkward. Gwen, meanwhile, is merrily eating her tea.

'Do you think you could stop looking at me like that?' Gwen asks mildly, after a few minutes.

'Like what?' I ask, startled.

'Like I'm an animal in a zoo.'

I flush. 'I'm sorry, I just... I never met anyone who was... that... before.'

'I think you'll find you have, they just didn't tell you. I can't imagine why.'

I find myself hastily thinking over my friends and

acquaintances.

'But... you're married to a man now?'

'Yes.'

'So... you don't like women anymore?'

Gwen sighs. 'Jess, like all married people, I sometimes encounter people other than my spouse whom I am attracted to and, were I single, might be interested in dating. The only difference is that, in my case, those people may be either male or female. Clear?'

'Okay.'

Gwen returns to eating. A few minutes pass by. 'You're doing it again.'

'I'm really sorry.'

'Where is it you're from again?'

'A little village up in the Dales.'

Gwen smiles wryly. 'Your own little bubble where everyone sticks to the mainstream and everything happens just like it's supposed to.'

'I suppose so.'

'The rest of the world isn't like that.'

An uncomfortable feeling floods me. I feel... insecure. 'No, I suppose not.'

I want to go home. I want my comfortable life back.

I get on my phone and buy Ryan a late birthday present. What did we ever do without Amazon wish lists? I try to phone, but I feel paralysed by the knowledge that I'm in the wrong. We never used to fight. At least not about anything major. Things just worked out for us. I don't know how to handle this situation.

I send him a text instead. He eventually replies, 'Doesn't matter.'

But does it?

Ben comes in while I'm watching TV, and I groan. 'Don't tell me, you want to watch the match.'

'Not really.'

I stare at him as he sits down on the sofa and puts his feet up on the coffee table. 'Really? Why not?'

'I don't like football.'

This does not compute.

'But you're a man,' I say, slightly bewildered. 'All men like football. Except if they're... you know.'

'Do I?'

I flush. 'Stop it.'

'The word is *gay*, Jess. It's only three letters and spelt quite phonetically.'

'Okay!' I snap. 'All blokes like football unless they're *gay*.'

Ben nods. 'Right. Now, watching football means hanging out with a load of other men watching a group of fit blokes run around in little shorts getting sweaty, right?'

'Yeah.'

'And what you're saying is, *not* wanting to do that makes a man gay?'

'I...'

When he puts it like that, it sounds pretty stupid.

'I'm going to tell you something that will blow your mind,' Ben says, leaning over and smirking at me. 'I'm straight and I don't like football and my brother's gay and he does.'

I turn away from him. 'Can you please stop making fun of me? I've already had this from Gwen.'

'Well, you do rather ask for it.' Ben gives my knee an affectionate squeeze. 'It's like you're from a different century. I know you live in a small village, but it can't be that backward. Does everyone there think like you?'

'I don't know, really.'

'Don't you ever get out of it?'

I shrug. 'Not much.'

'Uni?'

'I didn't go. I didn't want to get into debt and I wasn't that good in school anyway.'

'Travel?'

'I like home best. Plus, I've never really had the money.'

'Job?'

'Just the local council.' I feel a stab of nostalgia. 'It was a small office. We didn't deal directly with the public or anything. Most of the people lived close by. It was just... nice.'

Ben sighs. 'Seriously, Jess, you need your horizons expanded.'

'My horizons have been expanded quite enough, thank you,' I snap. 'Stuck here away from everyone, in a place where everything constantly changes, and I don't have any idea what's going to happen next. That's enough, without you all poking fun at me because I haven't had the same liberal upbringing as you.'

Ben holds his hands up. 'All right. I'll try not to tease.'

I feel tears pricking my eyes. 'How come you're always laughing about things? Don't you take anything seriously?'

'That's not fair,' Ben says sharply. 'Just because I don't mope around all the time doesn't mean I don't feel it.'

'Oh, so I mope, do I? Well, thanks a lot.'

I bolt off the sofa and stride out the door.

'Where are you going?'

'To mope in peace!'

A while later, there's a knock on my bedroom door.

'Sorry,' Ben says.

'It's okay,' I mutter. 'I'm sorry too.'

'Want a hug?'

'Yeah.'

Somehow the hug turns into a full body cuddle on my bed.

That's not cheating, right?

I've just said goodbye to Mum, and I'm trying to persuade the vending machine in the waiting room to give me something to drink, when Ben comes in, looking shattered.

'I think I've worked out why they restrict visiting hours so much,' he says. 'It's not to protect the babies; it's for the parents. There's only so many times you can face the same unanswerable questions. I think I'm going to start asking them back. I'll tell you when he's going to come home, if you tell me what the meaning of life is.'

'42.'

'Bad example.' He reaches over and presses the Coke button on the machine. It finally whirs into action. 'That's the only one working.'

'I don't like Coke.'

He reaches down and gets the can out. 'Fine, I'll drink this and get you something else from the shop.'

'Thanks.'

He strokes his goatee. 'Fancy another ride on the bike tonight? I feel like getting out for a bit, and I heard about a spot not far away that has some nice views over the area.'

I'm embarrassed to find myself actually flicking my hair, like I'm in a bad teenage romance. 'Yeah, okay. Might be nice.'

We walk out together pausing to put yet more gel on our hands and retrieve our stuff from the lockers.

We're passing through the doorway, and I'm just about to ask if he fancies grabbing some tea after the ride, when I hear, 'Jess!'

I start. It's Ryan.

He eyes Ben. 'Hi, I'm Ryan,' he says. 'Jess's fiancé.'

I don't know why he doesn't just pee against my leg.

'Nice to meet you,' Ben says. 'I'm Ben, my son is in the NICU with your daughter. See you later, Jess.' He strolls off towards the flats.

Ryan shoots a look of suspicion in his direction. I pretend I haven't seen.

'I got the present,' Ryan says. 'Thanks.'

'That's okay,' I say, hugging him. 'I'm sorry I forgot. All the days blur into one here and... Well, anyway. I'm sorry.'

'Doesn't matter.'

'Come to my room,' I say, taking his hand. 'That is, if you're not going to Neonatal?'

He fiddles with his watch. 'No, it's fine. Come on, let's go.'

So we go to my room. And we talk a little. And I apologise for forgetting his birthday, again. And I... well, let's just say I make it up to him.

And we're okay again. Mostly.

Two days later, I go in to see Samantha and she's on the CPAP again.

'How long this time?' I ask the nurse.

'Four hours and doing just fine.'

I look at her. The best way I can describe the setup is

that she looks like an elephant wearing a miner's helmet. She has a little mask over her nose with two big tubes coming off it that go to the CPAP machine. Those are held in place by big Velcro flaps on her white cotton hat. It is the most bizarre sight. But it's a whole lot better than a tube down her throat.

She's lying on her front, and she lifts up her head a bit and opens one eye. And, for the first time, she looks kind of cute.

Chapter 8

Samantha is now four weeks old and weighed in at 2lb 14oz this morning. After a couple of trials this week, she is now officially off the ventilator and onto CPAP!

Her feeding has also moved on a stage. Up until this week she has been fed continuously, keeping her little tummy full all the time. Now she gets a feed every two hours, so she's learning about feeling hungry - a big step towards proper feeding.

Tube feeding is a hateful way to feed a baby. Basically, you fill a syringe with one meal's worth of milk, attach the end to her feeding tube (by means of an irritating screw attachment my fingers can never seem to undo), hold up the syringe, use the plunger to give the milk a push, then take it out and let gravity do the work. It seems to take forever and it's amazing how quickly your arm starts to ache. I think I'm going to have to start lifting weights just to be able to do it without pain. Still, it's a big step forward for her. So I am glad. Also, hunger makes her a bit more alert just before a feed, which is lovely.

Four weeks and two days after I gave birth, I finally return home. Just for the day.

Mum and I live in a listed building. You're probably imagining an architectural gem. However, almost the entire village is listed with no more detail than 'there's a house here, and you're not allowed to knock it down'. It's in a terrace. The front is pebble-dashed and painted white, though it hasn't been that colour for some time. It has three floors: living room and kitchen diner on the bottom - kitchen at the back - my room, Amelia's old room and the bathroom on the middle floor and Mum's bedroom and en suite in what was once the attic. Its only historical value lies in being old. And, around here, even that isn't saying much.

It feels like I've been away for years. As we drive into the village - which is basically one street with houses either side - I look around for changes, and it seems crazy that I don't see any. I walk in through my front door, and there's a balloon with 'It's a Girl' written on it. I feel like breaking down. Because Samantha should have come home with me, and she hasn't.

'I'll put the kettle on, shall I?' asks Ryan, shifting awkwardly, and I nod so he'll go away. I force myself to unpack the pump which Ryan hired for me. It's a double of the ones they use at the hospital, though this one only has the basic setting rather than the special premature baby one. I eye it nervously. Please don't let one of the cats knock it over. This evil yellow machine costs £1300.

Ryan comes back through with a cup of tea. 'Your mum said there was somewhere she had to be, but she'll be back later. I've got the stuff in the steriliser,' he says, fiddling with his watch. 'Would you like a chocolate biscuit?'

I give him a weak smile. 'Thanks.'

He grins sheepishly back. 'I was talking to Donkey's missus and she reckoned you might like a foot spa while you're doing... that. So I got one. And the sales lady found some stuff to put in it. And she recommended a few other things as well, so...' He holds out a bulging carrier bag. 'I may have gone a bit overboard.'

'You think?' I laugh, taking the bag.

'Yeah, well. So... yes on the foot spa?'

'Yes,' I say, suddenly filled with love for him - and a twinge of guilt at the thoughts I've had lately. 'That sounds wonderful. Thanks, darling.'

He blushes slightly and disappears back into the kitchen. I open the bag and find stretch mark oil, bubble bath, nipple cream, face mask sachets and a world of other pampering. I just can't believe he did this. Not the shopping, but actually talking to someone - no, two people - about "women's stuff". And I didn't even know Donkey *had* a wife. Goodness, who would marry that prat? There's a reason he's nicknamed after an ass.

We sit together on the sofa, me on the pump with my feet in the foot spa - which is lovely - and Ryan eating Doritos, watching a DVD and holding hands. And, for the first time in months, I'm happy and I know why I wanted to marry him.

I never understood before that this could constitute romance.

At noon, I go to the doctor and manage to convince her to try me on Domperidone (the prescription drug for increasing milk supply), since the addition of Blessed Thistle doesn't seem to have done anything. Fingers crossed it will work. I don't know what I'm going to do if it doesn't. I can't keep leeching off Gwen. Ianto could be transferred down to Cardiff any day. And I don't know anyone else who would do that for me. Apparently, some places have milk banks, where mothers like Gwen with overactive mammary glands can donate their extra milk. I wish there was one around here, but there isn't. The postcode lottery strikes again.

I also get talked into trying a contraceptive implant. To be honest, I assumed that I would still be using the standard new mother method of contraception (i.e. a kitchen knife), but by this point I feel pretty much normal. So I'm booked in to have it fitted. At least then I won't have to worry about forgetting to take my pill. Not that I ever did.

I risk getting on the scales, and I'm thrilled to discover that I'm quite a few pounds lighter than I was before I went into hospital. Then it occurs to me that I no longer have a baby plus associated bits inside me, and that probably accounts for the difference. Oh well, at least I haven't gone up. My cousin Brenda went on and on about how breastfeeding meant you could eat anything you wanted and still lose weight. Then she got on the scales after six weeks, and she was heavier than before she gave birth. And she had a ten-pounder. Apparently, you could hear her screams of anguish in the next village. She shut up after that.

I have been trying. I live off the healthiest microwave meals that the Tesco Extra has to offer. I have resisted (mostly) the temptation of the hospital shop. I've walked nearly every day (I draw the line at heavy rain/snow). I'll just have to go along to Weight Watchers when I get home. Even if that will mean half the village knowing what I weigh.

'I invited the girls round this afternoon,' Ryan says over lunch. 'Your mum said it was fine. I thought you'd like to catch up.'

'Yeah... that's wonderful. What a nice idea.'

'And I'll just shove off to the pub and get out of your way.'

Oh, I see. There'll be a match on.

'Okay.'

We've just finished lunch when the first knock comes. After twenty minutes, the front room is filled with "the girls", sitting round and chatting. Ryan sneaks out and leaves me alone with them.

'Will you show us some photos of Samantha?' Martha asks. 'Laura says she actually looks like a baby now.'

'That's because she *is* a baby,' Laura says.

I hesitate. Their initial reaction rather puts me off. But these are my closest friends, after all.

Reluctantly, I get out my phone and scroll through my pictures, looking for the least threatening one.

Martha steals my phone and has a peek. 'Isn't she tiny?!'

Well, yes.

'What's that thing on her head?'

'Breathing apparatus. It blows air into her lungs to help her inflate them.'

'Oh.'

The phone gets passed around, and they start flicking through my other photos. I sit on my hands to stop myself grabbing the phone back.

'She looks sort of like a monkey, doesn't she?' Daisy asks.

I flinch.

Laura whacks her with a cuddly toy rabbit that's waiting for Samantha. 'You can't say that.'

'Oh, I wasn't being rude,' Daisy says quickly. 'She just does.'

'Once again, Daisy,' Laura says, rolling her eyes, 'saying that before you say something rude does not stop it being rude.'

'She kind of does, though,' Carol says. 'In a cute way.'

It's funny. I can admit to myself that she looks odd. Or, at least, not like a "normal" baby. But having other people say it - even my best friends - is like being stabbed.

I grab my phone back. 'Well, you're not supposed to see her at this point,' I say, as evenly as I can manage. 'It's like looking at a Yorkshire pudding halfway through cooking. Not that they look that good when they're done either, but you know what I mean.'

Part of me just wants to run upstairs and hide. Let them get on with their real lives. I barely remember mine.

'I think she looks like Ryan,' Martha says thoughtfully.

I take this as an attempt to make up for the monkey comment, rather than an actual judgement. I may have accused him of being an ape once or twice, but I didn't mean it literally.

'Shall we do presents now?' Laura asks.

General enthusiasm, which I try to join in with. I unwrap stuffed animals that Samantha can't play with, and clothes she's too small to wear, and try to act like I fit in. Until I'm forced to bring out the pump, which becomes an object of fascination.

'Can't you just pump what you need for the day in the morning?' Daisy asks.

If only.

'No. Breastfeeding works on a supply and demand basis, so you have to keep taking the milk out to get more. If I only pumped once a day, my milk would probably be gone in a week.'

'Doesn't that hurt?' Carol asks, prodding at the tubes my nipples are being sucked into.

'No. Not past the first few sucks anyway.'

And it doesn't *hurt*. It just... I don't know. It's uncomfortable. Not physically, but emotionally. I'm not sure I can explain it. Even if I tried, I'm sure no one would understand.

I have to answer questions all the way through, which really doesn't help me concentrate on milk production. At the end of the session, I take myself through to the kitchen to sort things out and store the milk in the fridge.

When I go back through, they seem to have forgotten about the pump. But they sit around talking about weddings, celebrities and soap operas and other things that have no meaning to me anymore. I've never felt so alone.

I find myself thinking about what Gwen said. About how I probably knew someone who was... different..., but they hadn't told me. This must be what it feels like to have something you feel you can't share, because people won't understand. I don't like it.

I find myself looking around my friends, searching for any clue that someone else is feeling left out.

'Girls,' I say awkwardly, when there's a lull in the conversation, 'can I ask you all something?'

General noises of assent.

'This is going to sound a bit odd,' I say, searching for the right words. Or, at least, not the wrong ones. 'Are any of you interested in women? You know... physically?'

Six pairs of eyes are now glued on my face, and six mouths are hanging open.

Claire recovers first. 'Er... is there something you wanted to tell us, Jess?'

I flush. 'No! I mean, no. I don't mean *I* am, I just...' I sigh. Gwen is right; I'm no good at this. I wouldn't blame any of my friends for not telling me. *I* wouldn't even tell me.

'Look, one of the other mothers at the hospital is... bisexual,' I say, wondering why I feel stupidly reluctant to say the word, 'and I found out and was a bit awkward. And I told her it was because I didn't know anyone who was. Or... gay. And she said that I probably did, they just hadn't told me because they thought I would be uncomfortable with it. And, to be honest, I am. But that's not the same as thinking it's *wrong*, it's just...' I sigh. 'I like things I understand. Things that are familiar. And stuff that isn't... rattles me.'

I look around, to see if I'm striking a chord with anyone. Nothing.

'What I wanted to say is: if anyone does... like women - or something else that's not... mainstream - you can tell me. I might be weird, but I'll work on it. And I won't stop being your friend. Well... actually if you like stabbing people or doing things to sheep, I might, but...'

I give up. 'You know what, never mind. Forget I said anything.'

I should have had Gwen write me a speech. Then it might have come out right.

'I don't think you'll ever make it as a public speaker, Jess,' Laura says. 'But that's okay. We still love you.'

I'm glad someone does.

After a few strange looks, the conversation goes back to reality TV and so forth, and, despite Laura's words, I find myself actually wishing I were back at the hospital.

When my friends have gone, I mope. Until Amelia comes round for a "chat" (read: abuse session).

'I was speaking to Marilyn at the church,' she says, by way of greeting, as she joins me at the kitchen table. 'And there's an opening next month. Had a cancellation. Apparently June's fiancé has left her for another man. I always knew she'd never keep him with those nails.'

I'm pretty sure that wasn't what did it.

I roll my eyes at the table. 'We're not getting married next month. I've got a mummy tummy to lose first, and Gwen says if I start doing stomach exercises before the muscles have knitted back together I'll end up looking like a Slinky.'

I'm sure Amelia has stiffened at the mention of Gwen's name.

'You remember Gwen?' I ask innocently. 'She has a baby in the NICU too. We're quite good friends. She was telling me about your hen holiday. Sounds like you had a lot more fun than you let on.'

Amelia pours herself a cup of tea. 'Oh, it was nothing. We sunbathed and danced a little. Just us girls.'

'You won't mind me seeing the photos, then? Gwen said she'd got some really... memorable... ones.'

'I can't imagine what of.'

We stare at each other across the table.

'Perhaps a month *is* a little soon,' Amelia says, dropping her gaze. 'I need time to find a suitable dress. I don't know what one is supposed to wear to a shotgun wedding.'

'Just a wedding, Amelia. Wear whatever you want.'

'I'll speak to Marilyn again and see if there's anything available later in the year. Perhaps September. There's still a good chance of nice weather and the flights should be cheaper.'

'I don't think we'll be taking Samantha on a plane.'

Amelia hesitates. 'I expect Mum and I could manage her for a few days.'

I gape at her. Has she just offered to do something *nice* for me? Gwen's photos must be seriously good.

'Well...' I say, feeling rather wrong-footed. 'That's... very kind of you. I'll... talk to Ryan about it.'

She avoids my gaze. 'No problem. And I'd really prefer you didn't see those photos. I had... really bad sunburn. And I left my sunglasses on, so I looked like a panda. I don't want anyone to see me like that.'

'Okay,' I say slowly, somehow resisting the urge to break into a wide grin. 'One good turn deserves another.'

Can I just say: I love blackmail.

Chapter 9

Once Amelia has disappeared back home, and Mum has returned, we potter about in companionable silence. I make a special effort to help with the housework, despite how knackered I feel, conscious of how much of my pregnancy I spent lying on the sofa.

I had a job when I got pregnant. Nothing terribly exciting, or glamourous. Or important, apparently, since I was made redundant. It seemed like a major blow then, but I suppose - given what's happened - it's worked out for the best. I can stay home with Samantha, and my redundancy pay and Ryan's contributions will keep us afloat until she's older and I can find a new job.

I'm pulling washing out of the machine, trying to find the detergent container - which has burrowed into the bundle again in its desperate attempt to escape its life of drudgery - when I come across something that shouldn't be there. Something I haven't seen since Dad died. A pair of men's pyjamas.

'Mum?' I yell over the vacuum cleaner. 'What are these doing here?'

Mum looks up from her work and freezes. Then she unfreezes, hastily turns away and mumbles something.

I watch her. She's deviating from her vacuuming pattern, which she has followed every Wednesday and

Saturday for as long as I can remember. Something is going on.

I finish extracting the washing - because she'll refuse to talk until I have - and then put the kettle on. This is a delicate matter and, as such, requires the right approach.

I bring her the tea as she turns off the vacuum cleaner and stows it carefully under the stairs.

'Do these pyjamas go on the racks, or should I tumble dry them?' I ask innocently.

Mum's cheeks are decidedly pink. 'Oh, I'll just pop them in the tumble dryer.'

'Did a friend stay over?'

'Yes, yes,' she says hurriedly, as she takes the pyjamas back into the kitchen. 'Long journey home.'

I watch her as she puts the pyjamas on the rinse cycle.

'So this friend,' I ask casually, putting the basket of washing on the stairs. 'Is he like... a boyfriend?'

'Don't be silly. I'm too old for that.'

What did they call boyfriends in the old days? 'But... a romantic interest?'

She doesn't answer. She turns the washing machine on. I reach over and stop it, then set it to dry and start it again.

'Because... that's okay,' I offer.

She looks up, startled. 'It is?'

If I'm honest, it's not totally okay. The thought of my mum being with anyone but my dad makes me vaguely nauseous. But she's my mum, and I want her to be happy.

'Of course! Dad's been gone a long time. If you've found someone else, that's... wonderful.'

She moves away and starts unpacking the dishwasher. 'It's just that it gets very lonely around here, especially with you living at the hospital. And all my friends have their own husbands and families. And... Howard's... lost his wife, and his kids are grown up. So we've been keeping each other company. It's really nothing.'

'It's nothing, but he's staying over?'

'It was just one time. He had a long journey home.'

'Yeah, you said that already,' I say, trying not to laugh.

Then the name registers.

'Wait... Howard? The guy with the beard, who looks like Brian Blessed?'

'There's nothing wrong with that,' she chides gently. 'He's very kind and gentlemanly.'

'Of course,' I hasten to say. 'I'm sure he's very nice. We'll have to have a chat the next time I'm in church.'

That is, if Amelia's theory isn't right and I don't get struck by lightning if I try to enter.

We look at each other awkwardly for a few seconds. Then, on impulse, I give her a hug.

We're interrupted by my phone alarm going off again. I get the strangest feeling of déjà vu.

'I have to pump again,' I say reluctantly, letting her go.

Mum watches me as I get things ready. 'You're doing really well,' she says. 'I'm proud of you.'

I keep facing the microwave so she can't see the tears in my eyes. 'Thanks, Mum.'

'Could you not tell Amy about this?'

I want to laugh. How ridiculous is it that we're both scared of what she thinks?

'Of course not, Mum,' I say. 'Your secret's safe with me.'

It's so nice to be at home. And that just makes me feel guilty. I should be missing Samantha desperately. But I'm not. I guess we haven't bonded yet.

I suppose that makes sense. There was no joy at her birth. I was still in shock, and she had to be whipped down to the NICU. I spent the rest of the day in the delivery room, waiting for a bed to come free on the postnatal ward, feeling largely forgotten about. Except for the nurse who came in with the knitted boob to show me how to do breast massage. That was possibly the most surreal experience of my life.

She was a week old before I held her, and I still can't do it very often. It took weeks before I was absolutely sure I hadn't just dreamt her early birth. I'm limited in what I can do for her, and there's a plastic box between us most of the time. We're separated a lot.

What if it never happens? Aren't you supposed to bond in the first three minutes? Her first three minutes were spent on a crash cart. What do we do if we never bond? How are we supposed to survive all the sleepless nights if we don't love each other?

And the nurses wonder why I don't ask questions. It's because there aren't any answers.

I head to Ryan's for tea and let myself in. He lives in what used to be the biggest house in the village, but is now divided into flats. The outside actually deserves its listing, but at some point in history the inside was pretty much gutted. I hope whoever did it got what they deserved, because it must have been spectacular in its day.

Ryan's flat is modern, in neutral colours because that's what it was like when he bought it and he isn't inclined towards interior decorating. It's full of surfaces that would be shiny if he bothered to clean them other than right before his mother comes round.

I go into the kitchen. He's actually set the table. There's a candle on it and everything. Admittedly, it's a novelty one that he got on holiday in the shape of a penis, but I suppose it's the thought that counts.

'It's almost ready,' Ryan says proudly. He's wearing one of those aprons with the body of a naked woman on it. 'Sit down and have a glass of wine.'

'Actually, I have to pump again.'

'Oh,' he says, looking deflated. 'Oh well, I can work around that.'

So we sit down on the sofa, to have what was apparently meant to be a romantic meal. Ryan tries dimming the lights - by which I mean he turns off the living room lights and leaves the kitchen one on - but that makes it too dark to see. So he brings the penis candle through and stands it up on top of a cardboard box. That sort of works. It's quite a big candle.

'So,' he says, giving me a grin, 'I have a plan.'

'Oh yes?' I cut up a piece of my chicken and pop it in my mouth.

'About our wedding.'

I instantly tense.

'See, I was thinking about how you don't want to live together before we get married, but you don't want to get married until you've got your figure back. I don't really see why, because I think you look fine, but my mum says it's totally normal, so fine.' He takes a deep breath. 'So, I've come up with a compromise, and I think it's really good.'

I stuff some rice into my mouth so I can get away with just nodding.

'So, here's my idea,' he says, putting his tray down and

turning to me. 'We go to the registry office as soon as they can fit us in and get married.'

'Ryan...'

'No, no, hear me out. We get married, just so we're married. We take a couple of your friends from the hospital along, so none of our family or friends have the advantage over the others. Then, once Samantha's at home and you're happy with your weight and everything, we'll have a proper wedding with everyone. Only we renew our vows instead of making them. We can even pretend to sign the register for the photos. Donkey's wife says you don't really sign it anyway, so it doesn't matter.'

He looks triumphant. 'That'll work, won't it? And we can even have a honeymoon. We can leave Samantha with your mother or mine...'

My head jerks up.

'... or take her with us,' Ryan adds quickly. 'I mean, she'll sleep lots, so we'll still have time to spend with each other.'

I put my head down again.

There's silence.

'So,' Ryan prompts after a minute, 'what do you think? It'll just solve everything, won't it?'

Yes, it will, damn him.

'I... I don't know.'

He frowns. 'What's wrong? Did I miss something?'

'I...'

Is there a good way to say, 'I'm just not sure I want to marry you anymore'?

Probably not.

'It's just,' I say, getting a germ of an idea, 'it's not really the same, is it? I don't think I'd feel properly married if we just had a quick five minutes in the registry office, even if it was legal. But then a vow renewal wouldn't really feel like a wedding either.'

Ryan's silent for another minute.

'Well... what do you need to feel properly married?' he asks. 'We could even sign a fake certificate at the vow renewal. I'm sure you could get a mock up. We'd get the registrar to come - maybe we could even get the same one. I'm sure lots of couples have done it. Like in that movie you liked. Um... the one with the singing.'

I stare at him. 'You'll have to be more specific.'

'The Indian one with the elephant.'

'*Bride and Prejudice.*'

'Right. They did it there. Had a quick ceremony to make it legal and then had the fancy wedding later. And they thought it was good enough. And over there you can't even be alone together if you're not married, can you?'

He may be right.

'I don't know. It's just...' I trail off.

There's nothing I can say. No excuse I can make. His plan is perfect. It solves everything.

'We'd have two wedding anniversaries,' I say lamely. 'That would be confusing.'

Ryan gets up suddenly. 'You don't want to do it because we would have two wedding anniversaries?'

I don't answer.

'The Queen has two birthdays. That works.'

I don't answer.

'Or is it just that you don't want to marry me?'

I try to say no, but can't seem to manage it.

'That's it, isn't it? You've changed your mind. After

ten years and a baby, *now* you don't think you want to marry me.'

I desperately want to turn back time. I may have thought this, but didn't want him to *know* about it.

'Ryan... I'm just confused,' I say. 'I'm under so much stress at the moment. I hardly sleep. I barely know which way is up. I don't know how I feel about *anything*. Please, please, please, can we just forget all this? Once Samantha's home and things go back to normal - well, sort of normal - I'll be able to sort my head out. Please?'

Will I? Will everything go back to normal?

Ryan slowly returns to the sofa and sits back down again. He picks up his tray and starts to eat. The silence stretches out.

'Ryan...'

'Fine,' he says. 'Fine.'

We eat the rest of the meal in silence.

Chapter 10

Ryan is giving me the one-word answer treatment, which is only one step up from the silent treatment. I head back home as soon as I can and beg a lift back to the hospital from Mum. As soon as we get there, we go see Samantha.

'We're going to move her into High Dependency later today,' the nurse says. 'One of the babies there is moving to Special Care, so there's space.'

High Dependency is the next step down from the NICU. It's a whole different room. Smaller and gentler.

'That's wonderful,' I say, fighting tears.

'It is,' Mum says, and gives me a hug.

'She's doing well,' the nurse adds kindly.

'I know.'

And I do. I know she's doing well. And I'm so grateful. But I'm still scared. I keep expecting to come in and be told that something has gone wrong. Surely, a baby can't be born so early and come out of it unharmed?

When I get to the common room, I find Gwen crying quietly on the sofa.

'What's wrong?'

She passes me her tablet without a word. I scan the article she's been looking at. There's a virus in the NICU at a hospital in Cardiff. One baby dead, three others seriously ill. Tension grips me. Those poor babies. Those poor parents. This is every NICU parent's nightmare come true.

Then realisation dawns. 'This is where Ianto was supposed to be born? Where you've been trying to get him transferred to?'

She nods.

I'm not sure what to say. I look at the article again. They're not sure what the virus is, or how it got in. Endless hand-washing and evil alcohol hand gel apparently haven't been enough.

'All this time,' she says, 'I've been ranting at Gareth about being stuck up here. How it's all his fault because he wanted to go on holiday and insisted it would be fine. And now... he might just have saved our baby's life. If Ianto was in that hospital right now, he could be sick, he could be dead...'

'But he isn't,' I interrupt hastily. 'He's okay. It all worked out. And I'm sure your husband understands. It's not easy being up here on your own, so far away from your family and friends.'

I'm lucky, really. Gwen lives so much further away from the hospital than I do. I know people who commute to work in this city every day.

'No, but it's a hell of a lot better than being down there would be right now. Makes you realise it could be so much worse.'

'Yeah,' I admit. 'It could be worse.'

Gwen wipes her eyes. 'I've told Gareth I'm staying up here until Ianto's ready to go home. I may be being silly, but this place has now saved his life twice over, and I'm not budging.'

'How did he take it?'

'He understands. Especially after my abject apologies for ranting at him all these weeks. It's not easy being apart, but... well, we've been through a few things together. We'll make it.'

I hand her another tissue and she wipes her eyes. 'Do you ever doubt that you belong together?'

Gwen smiles. 'No, never. Don't get me wrong, he drives me up the wall at times. But I know he's the one. Knew it the first time we met. And I miss him like crazy.'

'That must be nice. And horrible.'

'Yeah. Yeah, it is.'

Gwen and I head to Neonatal. I feel a desperate urge to hold Samantha.

'Ward round,' one of the nurses tells me, as we get to the door. 'Can you go and wait, please?'

What would happen if I refused? If I just ran in there and chained myself to her incubator?

I force myself to the waiting room.

Needing to hold your baby and not even being able to see her. This is what it is to be a NICU mum.

'Hey, you're back,' Ben says, when we meet in the corridor of the flats. 'What was it like going home?'

He's dressed head-to -toe in motorcycle leathers. It's a good look for him. I can't believe my heart is beating faster over a biker. If my mum knew about this, she'd lock me in my room.

'Strange,' I say, after a moment. 'Nothing's changed.'

'Weird, isn't it?'

'Very.'

'Fancy another ride? I was just heading out.'
'Sure.'

Soon I'm speeding around the streets again. Ben takes me up the nearest hill and we look out at the city lights together. It's beautiful. Quite romantic. And I find myself having dreams about him that I've only ever had about Ryan before.

I wish I knew what to do about them.

Chapter 11

Samantha is now five weeks old and has reached 3lb 2oz - almost a pound more than when she was born. She's already outgrown her first set of clothes. This week the doctors tried taking her off the CPAP machine and just giving her oxygen through a nasal cannula (a tube with two prongs that go into the nose). She managed ten hours before she ran out of energy. The doctors say it's a good start.

I think I'm making a little more milk. But maybe I'm imagining it. The doctor said it would take the drugs a week or so to kick in. I'm just so desperate for it to work. Rationally, I know Samantha would probably cope fine on formula. But I already feel like I've failed her once by not being able to keep her inside me. I need to do this. Whatever it takes.

After days of debating with myself, I decide to talk to Gwen about Ben. I can't talk to my friends back home. One, because they don't understand what life is like here. Two, in a village nothing stays private.

She's in her room, which is unusual. She hangs out in the common room when she's not in Neonatal. Her hair looks mussed when she answers the door. She rubs a hand over her face.

'Sorry, were you sleeping?'

'No, just hiding under the duvet.'

'Oh.' I shift in the doorway. 'Can I come in? I really need to talk about something.'

Gwen sighs. 'Sorry, Jess, but not right now.'

'But it's really important,' I say. My bottled up feelings are ready to burst free, like anything fizzy when you shake it.

'Flipping hell, Jess, I said not now!' she snaps. 'I need some time to myself. I'm not the bloody Samaritans!'

I'm stung into silence. She shuts the door in my face.

I suddenly feel completely helpless. I hadn't realised how dependent I'd become on her to be the strong one. I need to reach out to someone, and there's no one there. Ryan's still smarting over my rejection of his two-stage wedding idea.

Is it fate or Sod's Law that brings Ben into the flats at that moment? And back into my bed. Just to cuddle. Just as friends.

I think.

Our cuddle is interrupted by my phone ringing. It's Ryan. I suddenly feel horribly guilty and quickly get up and sit on the chair. Ben props his head up on his elbow and listens.

'Guess what?!' Ryan says, before I can get a word in.

'What?'

'You're talking to the new depot manager at Daltons!'

'What?' I say again, feeling disorientated.

'I've been promoted! Keith's retiring at the end of the month and I've landed his job. They just told me!'

'That's wonderful.'

I do try to sound happy. I really *am* happy for him. I'm just so unhappy for me right now that I can't put it across.

There's a momentary silence. 'That's it?'

'No, it really is wonderful,' I try again. 'Sorry, Ryan. It's just today has been a really bad day and...'

'And when's the last time you had a good one? Bloody hell, Jess, is it too much to ask for you to put stuff aside for two minutes?'

'Our daughter is not *stuff*. And no, I can't. And I don't understand how you can just forget about her whenever it suits you.'

'I don't *forget* about her. I put my issues aside so that I can get on with what needs to be done. We can't all drop everything and wallow.'

'I'm *wallowing* now?!'

'Fine, not *wallowing*, but...'

'Oh, forget it! You just don't understand, do you? Well, okay, get back to your life. And I am glad you got that promotion, because at least it means you'll have more money to pay child support!'

I hang up on him. He calls right back, but I refuse to answer.

'I think I'd better go,' Ben says, rolling off the bed and heading back to his own room.

My phone tells me I need to pump again and I feel a desperate urge to throw it out the window and just hide under the duvet like Gwen.

Ryan calls seven more times in the next two hours. I don't answer a single one. And I know I'm being childish, but I can't summon up the energy to be anything else.

I'm silently eating tea in the common room, later that night, when Gwen and Cassandra come in.

I suddenly notice that Cassandra has toned down her appearance since we first met. She seems to have given up on the manicures, and the makeup has gone down to the bare bones. It's rather nice, seeing as I haven't worn makeup since week seven of pregnancy.

'Hi, Jess,' Gwen says, smiling wryly. 'I knocked on your door earlier, but didn't get an answer. I'm sorry about earlier.' She pulls a bar of chocolate out of her smock pocket and hands it to me. 'You caught me at a really bad time.'

'That's okay,' I say awkwardly. I remember the knock. I'm so glad she didn't persist. 'I'm sorry I bothered you.'

'Oh, Jess, you don't bother me,' Gwen says, sliding into the chair next to me. 'I want you to come to me. I want to be here for everyone. It's just... every so often it all gets on top of me and I hide, you know? And I really can't take visitors then. I come out of it on my own, given a bit of time.'

Cassandra sits down on my other side and steals a piece of the chocolate.

'I guess you always seem so together. And you've done all this before. I forgot it's hard for you too.'

Gwen shrugs. 'People always do. Some even tell me what a comfort it must be to have had one healthy premature baby. And in some ways it is. I know what to expect, and I know a happy ending is possible - even likely. But still...'

She twists her curls around her finger absent-mindedly. 'Sometimes I can't help worrying that I've used up all my luck. Like Anwen being healthy means that Ianto must have something wrong with him to balance it out.'

'I've never thought of it like that.'

Cassandra is nodding. 'I know what you mean.'

I can't help wondering if she's right. I mean, all in all I've been pretty lucky. I live in a nice house. We've always had enough for the essentials and some treats as well. I have a nice fiancé - I think. Friends. I'm healthy. Was Dad dying young enough to balance that out, or am I due some more bad luck?

'I don't think it works like that,' I say. 'I mean, some people are always lucky and some are terminally unlucky. I don't think the whole balance thing works on an individual basis. It's on a bigger scale.'

'I expect you're right,' Gwen agrees. 'And Lord knows there's no point in fretting about it. Anyway, what was it you wanted to talk to me about?'

I open my mouth. Then I shut it again. I'm not sure I want Cassandra knowing about Ben. I'm not even sure now that I want Gwen knowing. Maybe it's better just keeping it to myself.

There's nothing to tell really. We're just friends.

'It doesn't matter,' I say. 'It... sorted itself out.'

'Funny how things do that sometimes.'

'Yeah.'

'You know what, I think we need to escape,' Gwen says, looking around. 'We're all going crazy cooped up round here. Fancy a day at the seaside?'

Cassandra and I look at her like she's gone nuts.

'I'm serious!' she says. 'We've all got hire pumps. I know everything we'll need. Cassandra, you get your husband to drop off the SUV and take the bus to work, and we'll pack up and go.'

Cassandra looks as sceptical as I feel.

'Honestly, it is possible. I've pumped in a zoo before.

And an amusement park. I tried it in the back row of a cinema once, but they threw me out for making too much noise.' She bounces in her seat. 'Come on, we need to get out! Tesco and Mothercare do *not* count as diversions, and we need to have some fun. It's a mental health thing.'

'I'm in,' Cassandra says suddenly. 'Sod it. You're right. Let's go.'

'It's February,' I protest. 'It'll be freezing.'

'So wear a big jumper, and we'll use the seat heater. I wasn't suggesting we go skinny dipping. Although, that is a great laugh. I did it once on holiday and came back married.'

'I thought you met your husband at a rugby match?' Cassandra asks, brow furrowing.

'Oh, it wasn't to him, this was someone else. Long story.'

I'm starting to think that she may actually be serious when she says things like that.

A few days later, it's sunny and relatively warm and Gwen declares us ready. I'm already in a good mood, because by now I'm positive my milk supply is increasing and the relief is overwhelming.

Cassandra drives us to the nearest point on the coast, which is Redcar. It's not exactly a tropical paradise, even in summer. When they filmed the movie *Atonement*, they used the beach here to stage the D-Day landings. It's hardly a ringing endorsement. There's heavy industry at one end, a wind farm out to sea, and huge ships can be seen on the horizon.

Though, to be fair, it isn't a bad beach. It's sandy, long and wide - especially when the tide is out. I have happy memories of playing here when I was small. When the sea seemed as far away sitting at the top of the beach as it did at home. Picking up shells and driftwood - and a good few lolly sticks along the way. Amelia and I used to build sandcastles and decorate them with bits of dried-out seaweed, then run around with kites. That and kick sand at each other and throw tantrums over dropped ice creams. Eventually, Dad would get sick of it all and announce it was time to go. After some negotiation, we would compromise and walk down the front to the shops to get fish and chips for tea. Then we would drive home, shoes full of sand and clothes covered in ice cream and chip grease, and fall asleep in the car.

This time, we all sit in the car and pump. Gwen insisted it was possible to pump while driving, but Cassandra refused to try. I'm in the back and in charge of the pumping gear. We pass round wipes and alcohol hand gel and then I get out our steriliser tanks. Gwen has provided three tubs with clip on lids, labelled with our names in her loopy handwriting. I can't believe how organised she is.

Cassandra holds her tank up and looks at the floating pump bits. 'It's rather like a fish tank.'

'Lesser spotted flanges, tube fish and the little known rubber membranes,' says Gwen.

We sit together; the pumps merrily chewing up batteries. Gwen retunes the radio every time a song ends, driving us all crazy. Cassandra stares at nothing and I start re-reading *Pride & Prejudice*.

'We should sing,' Gwen says. 'Maybe "Sisters are Doing it for Themselves".'

We groan and roll our eyes.

'Seriously! It's fun. I'll start...'

She's just belting out, 'it's no longer true' when there's a rap on the car window and we all jump.

Heads swivel in that direction. There's a police woman standing there. Cold dread floods me. I can't get arrested. Is pumping in a public car park illegal?

Cassandra winds down the window. Gwen gives the police officer a big grin. Cassandra and I smile nervously.

'Hi, officer,' Gwen says. 'Can we help?'

The police woman looks a bit stunned. 'Er... no. A couple of members of the public mentioned a black SUV with tinted windows had pulled up, and no one had got out. I was just checking nothing was wrong.'

'It does look quite intimidating, Cassandra,' Gwen says cheerfully. 'All it needs is "Torchwood" stencilled on the side.'

'My husband wouldn't let me,' Cassandra says, with a small smile.

'What's *Torchwood*?' I ask, still nervous.

'TV show. You wouldn't like it. Although I might show you an episode or two as part of your education. Anyway...' Gwen leans towards the window. 'We're fine, officer. We're all pumping for our babies, who are in the hospital because they were born early. We've just come to Redcar to remind ourselves that the outside world still exists.'

'Oh, well, that's fine then. Er... is there anything you need?'

Cassandra and I quickly shake our heads.

'You couldn't get us some ice creams, could you?' asks Gwen.

Gwen was right about needing to get out. As we walk back to the car after our trip into town, I feel lighter than I have in weeks.

I don't know if I can express what I feel like right now, but I'll try. Can you imagine wearing something skin tight and too small, that covers your whole body? You can still function, but you feel a constant pressure all over, all the time. Now imagine staying like that for weeks. After a while, you start to be afraid you will eventually be crushed.

It's partly the sleep-deprivation, I suppose. And partly making milk, which takes it out of you more than you'd believe if you haven't done it yourself. But mostly, it's the fear. The unending, swarming fear that something is going to go wrong. That you'll go in to see your baby and she won't be there anymore. And no matter how well they're doing, it never goes away.

Maybe every new mother feels that fear. Maybe it's only amplified in the NICU.

I'm sure some people won't understand how you can go out and enjoy yourself when your baby is in hospital. The answer is that you have to, because if you let the fear overwhelm you, you'd run away.

I know that, and yet I rail at Ryan for doing the same thing. I suppose I'm just using it as an excuse to push him away. I told him the truth, I don't know how I feel about anything anymore.

'I'm going to go and paddle,' I say.

Gwen and Cassandra exchange looks. 'The tide's out. It's about a two mile walk to the sea,' Cassandra points out.

I shrug. 'Don't care. I'm going. You coming?'

Somehow, we all end up paddling. And it is indeed freezing.

When we get back to the hospital, everything feels better. I make it into the corridor of the flats when I hear a loud exclamation of 'Arse!' from the kitchen.

'Hey, Jess. I think I broke the microwave,' Ben greets me. 'Who knew you couldn't use it to dry trainers?'

'Everybody. You didn't seriously do that, did you?'

'No, just asked it to defrost something. Apparently, that isn't in its job description.'

'Of course not.' I smile at him.

He smiles back. 'You're in a good mood.'

'I am.' I hand him a stick of rock. 'We've had a girls' trip to the seaside.'

'In February?'

'Strange, but true. We even paddled. And now life doesn't seem so bad.'

'Oh, well then,' Ben says, chucking his half-defrosted ready meal in the bin. 'Fancy going out for dinner?'

It's amazing how exotic a carvery can seem when you're living in the hospital. Maybe that's why the nurses keep going on about it.

Ben and I run across the road just as the lights change, holding hands like a couple of teenagers. Though, admittedly, in my teenage years I never felt the need to tighten my pelvic floor muscles just in case.

'So, Edward's mother, what's her name?' I ask, in a hopeless attempt at subtlety, when we've got our food.

'Marie.'

'When does she get back from... where was it?'

'Mauritius. She's back already.'

'Oh.' I frown at him. 'I must have missed her coming in.'

Ben pours gravy over his meat. 'No, you didn't.' He pulls a face. 'It's a bit complicated. She... doesn't want to be involved. It's just me and him.'

I'm stunned. 'Not involved? How can she not be involved? He's her son. She just gave birth to him.'

'Like I said, it's complicated.'

'But...' I scramble for something to say. 'You said she named him. That's got to mean she's a tiny bit interested. Right?'

He shrugs. 'I thought so, actually, when she said it. Thought maybe the maternal instincts were kicking in. But it hasn't led to anything.' He cracks his knuckles. 'Maybe something'll happen. If I'm lucky. Or unlucky. Who the hell knows?'

'What's she like?'

This seems to require thought. 'Nice, I guess,' he finally comes up with.

I'm trying to grapple with the idea of someone describing their newborn's mother this way, when he interrupts my thoughts. 'What about your fiancé?'

'Oh... he's wonderful,' I say, realising as I do that I sound no more enthusiastic than he did. 'I mean... I've spent six months wanting to smack him and the last few weeks feeling abandoned, but everyone feels like that, don't they?'

I force a laugh.

He doesn't look terribly convinced. 'Wouldn't know. Maybe they do. He's nice, though, right?'

'Yeah. Yes. I mean, we've been together ten years and, until this happened, we were really happy.'

'Ten years... wow. And you haven't got married yet?'

I point my fork at him. 'Don't you start. I get enough

of that from my mum. And my sister. I'm still only 25, you know.'

'That's what's holding you back?'

'Yeah. I guess.'

'But you're old enough to have a baby?'

I flush. 'We didn't actually plan that.'

'Ah.'

'Was Edward planned?'

'Hell no. No one I know with kids planned them.'

'Everyone I know did.'

He laughs. 'What century are you from?'

'This one! I just have nice friends, that's all.'

'So anyone who doesn't plan their kids isn't nice?'

'I didn't mean that,' I say. 'I just meant... my friends are responsible. Mature.'

'Are you?'

'What?'

'Responsible and mature?'

'Well,' I shift awkwardly, 'yeah.'

Though I don't know that I've been acting like it lately.

'And yet you've had an unplanned pregnancy. Which rather ruins your theory.'

I start shredding my napkin. 'Oh, you know what I mean.'

He takes a slurp of his drink. 'Obviously, I don't.'

'Well, I'm engaged.'

'And that makes it all right?'

'Well... better.'

'So, if it had happened right before you got engaged it wouldn't have been?'

'Well... not as good, but we would have just got engaged anyway.'

'So the ring makes the difference, even though you would be exactly the same people without it?'

'I... yes.'

'You're definitely not from this century,' he says, stabbing a carrot.

I stare at him angrily. 'There's nothing wrong with traditional values. Don't you think it's best for a child to be planned, and their parents committed to each other?'

He stares right back. 'Sure. I just don't like the assumption that anything other than that is bad. Life doesn't always work out neatly. Shit happens, and the measure of a person is whether or not they stick around to clean it up.'

I glare at him. 'Is this your usual dinner conversation?'

'Do you have rules about that too?'

'Most people call them manners.'

'So good manners mean you can't have a difficult discussion over food? Does it only apply to full meals, or would a bag of crisps count?'

I open my mouth and then close it again. 'Do you have to make fun of me?'

He grins, instantly lightening the mood. 'No, but it's kind of fun. Plus, if it'll get you to loosen up, it's a good thing. With that in mind, fancy a glass of something alcoholic?'

'I can't, it'll get into the milk. I'm responsible, remember? And mature?'

'If you say so,' Ben says. 'Could we compromise on some Bailey's cheesecake?'

'I expect so.'

'All right then.' He holds up his glass. 'Happy Valentine's Day.'

Oh, no. Don't tell me I forgot that as well.

I whip out my phone and send Ryan a quick text. We've reconciled somewhat, though things are still... distant. And I still don't know how I feel about that. A minute or two later, he sends one back.

'Another drink?' asks Ben.

Chapter 12

Samantha is now six weeks old and weighed in at 3lb 6.5oz on Friday. She has had her six week brain scan and everything looks normal. A couple of days ago, they tried taking her off CPAP again. This time, she coped just fine. In fact, a day later she took out her nasal cannula and started sucking on it, with no apparent ill effects. It's taped on more securely now.

It's official. I am now making enough milk to feed Samantha. In addition, I'm starting to fall out of my nursing bra; fantastic! I report back to the doctor when I go to have my contraceptive implant fitted and come close to falling at her feet in gratitude. Finally, my breasts are doing what they're supposed to.

But my thoughts keep straying to Ben. Over dessert in the restaurant, it really felt like we bonded. I keep imagining what it would be like to kiss him.

Maybe Ben is the one for me. People keep going on about 'everything happens for a reason'. Maybe they're right. Maybe this whole thing had to happen just so I'd meet Ben. I mean, how many people marry someone they met when they were fifteen?

Ben and I could get married and set up home together. And we have a boy and a girl, so we'd be an instant family. We'll go round Tesco together, and people will say, 'Oh, are they twins?' And we'll smile at each other tenderly and explain the crazy story of how we met...

Of course, nothing's going to happen until we get out of here. But then we'll keep in touch. Get to know each other via text and Facebook. Meet up occasionally. And love will slowly blossom...

I shouldn't be thinking like this.

On the pump the next day, I get hit by another random wave of fury.

This is *not fair*. Everything is *not fair*. What did I do to deserve this? What did *Samantha* do to deserve this? Everyone I know has normal pregnancies and normal babies. Why do I have to go through this? My life was chugging along quite happily and then - wham bam, thank you ma'am - I got knocked up, had a miserable pregnancy, lost my job and then gave birth to a scrawny alien who couldn't even breathe for herself. I hate *everything*.

Once I'm finally done with pumping, I stride back to the flats. I feel the anger boiling inside me, and I just don't know what to do about it. But then, I was reading this article a while back that said that all this about letting anger out is wrong - it just reinforces it - and actually we should all be British and suppress it. Who even knows? Every time you think you understand something, someone does a new study and it turns out you don't.

I have to wait to enter the flats because someone is coming out. A pretty, chubby blonde of about 16. I steam quietly while she minces past on her stupidly high heels.

'Hey, Jess,' Ben says wearily, as I pass the common room. 'How's your day been?'

'Lousy.'

'Mine too. Edward's mother's just been. You must have passed her on the way out.'

I do a double take. '*That's* his mother? She's a child!'

'She's not a child, she's nineteen.' Ben sighs. 'Allegedly.'

'You were actually *dating* her?'

'Not exactly.'

'What does that mean?'

'It's complicated.'

I snort. 'Seriously, Ben, how did you end up in this situation?' I snap. 'You don't like her, you barely even seem to know her.'

'You don't want to know.'

'Don't tell me what I want!'

Ben gets up and marches over to the window, then spins back to face me. 'You want the truth? I met her in a club at my mate's stag party. We were both rat-arsed and slightly stoned. We screwed each other in a toilet cubicle and we were both too out of it to use a condom. It wasn't my finest hour, all right?'

I feel slightly sick. 'That's it? That's how your son was conceived?'

Ben turns back, cracking his knuckles. 'Look, not everyone has the perfect life like you. Some of us fuck up. If it makes you feel any better, I've had to pay for it. First, I had to get tested for STIs. Which, among other things, involved getting a cotton bud stuck up my cock, which is not something I care to repeat. Then I had to talk her out of an abortion, which was a laugh. And when I succeeded I had to go with her to tell her parents, which went so well her dad and brother beat me up. And I mean badly. I've spent months shitting myself over becoming a single dad, and that was when I was expecting a healthy kid.'

He lets out a shuddering breath. 'Now I have a son born so early he was only borderline viable. They keep trying to take him off the ventilator, but he can't seem to manage on his own and honestly I'm worried he may spend the rest of his life on it. And now, to top it all off, I find out that his own mother actually *tried* to induce premature labour.'

I feel sick. 'You can't be serious.'

'Fuck, I wish I wasn't.'

'So that's why he was born early?'

He shakes his head. 'I don't know. Maybe it was. Maybe her attempts failed, and it was just coincidence. But it's the fact that she tried... I could have dealt better with an abortion. I don't even want to let her see him knowing that, but I suppose I'll have to if she asks. Honestly, I'm at the point of hoping she won't. Maybe I'll tell him she died. I'm obviously not going to tell him the truth. It's not exactly a fairy tale.'

I reach out awkwardly and put a hand on his shoulder. 'Look, I'm sorry. I didn't mean to judge. Or... I guess I did, but I wish I hadn't. Life... well, it's always been simple. Around where I live, with the people I know. Gwen thinks I live in a bubble, and I'm starting to think she's right.'

'I'd say so.'

'I liked my bubble,' I confess, blinking back tears. 'I knew what my life would be like. It was all going to plan. And then I got pregnant, and it all went wrong. I don't have the perfect life. I have nothing in common with my friends anymore. My sister acts like this is all my fault. Everyone's obsessed with planning my wedding, and as for

Ryan... I'm not even sure I want to marry him anymore. Sometimes he can be so sweet and sometimes he's so ruddy dense I just want to smack him and... I just don't know anymore...'

'Hey,' he says, pulling me into a hug. 'Look, we'll both get through it, all right? Life sucks now, and we're going through hell, but we just have to keep going and we'll get out the other side.'

'Thanks,' I say, slightly muffled by his shoulder. I lift my head, intending to kiss his cheek. He turns his head and for a moment I think he's going to kiss me on the mouth. But he doesn't.

Chapter 13

I walk into High Dependency and Samantha isn't there.

Fear grabs me and I can't breathe. For a moment, the world goes grey and ice cold.

Fortunately, the nurse grabs me before I have a chance to move onto a full blown panic attack.

'She's been moved!' she says. 'One of the Special Care babies went home yesterday and the night doctor decided to move Samantha. She's been ready for a week, really, we just haven't had the space.'

Sometimes, I want to scream at the doctors and nurses. I'm so grateful for the care they give Samantha, but I feel so pushed out of her life. I'm her mother and yet I'm so often the last to know what's happening with her. Don't they realise that an empty cot where their baby should be is every mother's worst nightmare?

'That's wonderful!' I say, even though it feels more frightening than anything. 'Well... take me to her.'

And so I'm taken through the mystical door to Special Care.

It's another world. Coming in there's a sink - of course - and then a much smaller reception desk with a little office behind it. There are two rooms to the left and then more off a corridor to the right. There are murals painted on the wall, like you get in children's libraries. The lights are softer. The beeping is quieter.

'We've put her in here for now,' the nurse says, showing me to one of the rooms on the left.

Her room still doesn't have any windows, but to make up for that someone's painted one. It looks out over a farm. A farm with teddy bears. And underneath the window is Samantha... in a cot. An actual cot. Admittedly, it's a clear plastic one that looks like a really deep cat litter tray, on top of a cupboard with wheels on it, but it's still *a cot*!

'She's in a cot,' I say stupidly.

The nurse smiles. 'She can regulate her own temperature now. She's been at room temperature in the incubator for a while. Just think how much easier it will be to change nappies now you don't have to put your hands through the incubator holes!'

I look at her, sleeping. 'What do I... I mean, what's my role here?'

'Mum.'

I probably sound stupid. I wish the nurses could understand that I don't know what that means. I'm a first time mum, and I haven't even had a chance to be that. 'I know, but... what can I do? Like... can I pick her up?'

'If you want.'

'How often?'

I think this nurse is actually getting it. 'Whenever you want, honey,' she says sympathetically. 'She's not in the NICU now. I know she's small, but she's not far off being like any other newborn. She should *want* to be held. Her oxygen tubes are attached to the wall, so I'm afraid you can't wander round with her, but they'll stretch to the chair so you can sit and hold her. If you're worried about anything, just shout for help.'

'That's wonderful,' I say, trying to blink back tears. This time I mean it.

'I usually advise not picking up a sleeping baby, though,' she adds, with a wry smile. 'Some of them really don't like to be disturbed. She's used to sleeping by herself - and, believe me, you want to encourage that!'

Right now, I think if she wanted to spend the next five years sleeping on me that would be fine. But I suppose I'll feel differently further down the line.

'I'll give you a bit of time to get settled in,' she says, 'and then I'll show you around the rest of the place.'

'Thanks.'

I stand by Samantha, looking down at her. I can just see her and it's not through plastic. She makes noises that I've never heard before. Not bad noises, just... baby noises, I guess. The plastic and the beeping monitors must have drowned them out before.

She has her nasal cannula in and the sticky patches that help hold the tubes onto her face, but she's close to looking like a normal baby now. There's still something about her face that is a little off, but I can't put my finger on what. The books call it the "preemie look" and say it wears off in time. She's wearing a little babygro and a hand-knitted cardigan and has an amazingly deep pile of blankets over her. The top one is simply knit in rainbow wool.

Her monitor beeps and I jump. I hadn't registered until now that it was silent. I watch the stats for a while. It seems to be set to only beep below 75% blood oxygen. She drops down and then goes back up all the time. But I'm used to it now.

I really wish I'd had more warning about this. It's like going into work and finding out you've been moved to a new office. Even if it's a nicer one, it's still horribly unsettling. I don't do well with change when I don't have time to adjust first.

I stand there staring at her for a while. And I hold her hand, just because I can.

Chapter 14

Samantha is now seven weeks old. After weeks of slow and steady weight gain, she has shot up this week and is now 4lb 1oz!!! She has started to learn how to drink from a bottle. The first time she got a bit of milk down the wrong way, but, once she recovered, she managed to have half her feed like that. She's had another try today and managed a bit more. Before she can go home, she needs to be off oxygen and be taking all her feeds from breast and/or bottle instead of the tube. To do this she just needs to grow - to get bigger and stronger. So, we wait.

I was going through some of her stuff, and I found one of her first tiny nappies and thought, 'She didn't really fit into that, did she?' Already I'm starting to forget.

Ben is just heading out in his running gear when I get back from pumping.

'It's raining,' I say.

He zips up his jacket. 'I know, but I have to get out. I can't stay still, and I can't do nothing.'

'What's the matter?'

'Edward.' Ben cracks his knuckles. 'He's still not off the ventilator. They reckon he needs his heart thingy fixed before he'll manage it, but the ibuprofen hasn't worked. They're sending him up to the RVI for heart surgery.'

I feel cold. 'When?'

'Tomorrow.'

I grab his hands. 'It'll be okay,' I say, as convincingly as I can. 'They do this all the time. And once they get that fixed, things should get better for him.'

'That's the hope,' Ben says gruffly. 'Look, I've just... got to go.'

He moves out of my grasp and jogs off down the corridor. I see him rub his arm roughly across his face.

Overnight, I notice that my breast looks red and feels warm. I consult my breastfeeding book, which suggests mastitis, which is caused by a blocked milk duct. Wonderful. Over the course of the day, it becomes harder and redder. I call my GP for an appointment. I try to avoid taking painkillers, but by evening I've caved. The book stresses the need for rest (why does everything require the one thing that's hardest to get?), fluids and breast massage to unplug the duct. I cannot tell you how painful that is.

I give into temptation and raid the hospital shop. I'm comforting myself with chocolate and a hot water bottle borrowed from Gwen when Ben calls.

'Is it over?' I ask. 'How's Edward?'

'He's fine,' Ben says, his voice full of relief. 'It's over, it all went fine. We'll be back in a day or two.'

'Oh, that's wonderful!' I say, with more joy than I've felt in weeks. 'And hopefully that will make things better for him.'

'Should do,' Ben says. 'But honestly, right now I'm just glad it's over.'

I try to imagine Samantha being operated on. It makes my insides freeze up. 'Yeah, I can understand that.'

'Anyway, I'm going to get back to him. I just wanted to let you know. Tell the others.'

'I will.'

I guess, actually, mastitis isn't too much to bear.

The doctor confirms I have mastitis. I get the antibiotics, and in a few days things have gone back to normal.

'It's probably about time we start trying her on the breast,' the nurse says, when I'm sitting by Samantha's cot. 'At least, if you want to. You're pumping, aren't you?'

I grin. 'Oh yes. Can we, really?'

I get set up in the armchair with my breastfeeding pillow on my lap and the nurse hands Samantha to me. Gingerly, I manoeuvre her until her mouth is in the right place and try to put her onto my nipple.

'You need to get more of it into her mouth. Like this.'

The nurse shoves far more of my boob than there's room for into her mouth. I'm not sure if this is latching. I am sure that it *hurts*.

I sit there, rigid. My shoulders are aching. And she is chewing on me.

'Are you *sure* she doesn't have any teeth?' I ask warily.

The nurse laughs. Because it's so hilarious. 'No teeth. We can try with a nipple shield. The little ones often find it easier to feed like that.'

A shield sounds really good. Preferably made of some sort of iron.

'Okay.'

The nurse brings me what is essentially a bottle teat made to fit over my nipple. And it does help. By which I mean, her invisible teeth are no longer sinking into me. And she isn't pulling away and screaming, so I presume she's getting milk.

I sit there, doing what I've been waiting nearly eight weeks to do, thinking, 'How long do I have to do this for?'

I assumed that breastfeeding would be this lovely bonding experience. That's what kept me going all these weeks on the pump. I just had to keep the milk supply going until she could feed properly. But, the truth is, it's just someone sucking on my nipple. And, unlike all those Mills & Boon heroines who practically orgasm on the spot, I've never liked that. When Ryan's tried it, I've always pushed him away. Or suppressed the urge for his benefit. It just... makes me feel bad.

Maybe my whole body is faulty. This is no better than pumping. In fact, it's worse. Because I can hate the pump freely, and I don't want to hate her. I just want to pull her off me.

I wonder how many illusions I have left to shatter.

Chapter 15

Samantha is now eight weeks old and weighs 4lb 11oz and a bit. This week she had her first set of vaccinations, and an eye test. She'll get another eye test on Wednesday, because the blood vessels behind her right eye aren't fully formed yet. At the moment, they look fine. Which is wonderful, because many babies who have spent three weeks on the ventilator will have over-developed ones that can cause vision problems. Or something like that. The important thing is that her eyes look fine. The physiotherapist came to observe her and wasn't worried. She'll have a proper examination later on.

The nurses say she's generally much more vocal at feed times. One day I suspect I will look back at my diary entries about how I wished she could cry and laugh.

Do you have any idea how long it takes to heat up enough sterile water to fill a baby bath? It comes in tiny bottles, like Yakult, so it's a long time. And Samantha entirely defeated the object by pooping in said bath.

I felt about as qualified to bathe Samantha as I do to handle an electric eel. Somehow, I managed to lay her along my arm and keep her steady while I washed her with the other hand, praying all the time for her not to wriggle. I was so glad there was a nurse there. I have no idea how parents do this without one.

'What's a nurse-in?' I ask.

'Well, basically,' Gwen says, flopping down on the sofa, 'it's where a bunch of women sit around and breastfeed their babies, in a probably futile effort to convince a load of narrow-minded pricks that doing what nature intended is normal. Plus, it's a chance to get your tits out in public and I always like that.'

'But we're not breastfeeding,' Cassandra says.

'We are. Just with the help of an intermediary. I don't see any reason why we can't make it a pump-in too. Loads of people don't even know it's possible to pump full-time. It's really important to raise awareness.'

Cassandra and I exchange glances. Honestly, I'm not sure I want to promote this as a feeding method.

'Come on! At least it's a change of scenery.'

I never thought I'd see the day when going topless in a shopping centre would constitute an outing.

'I'll go if you will,' Cassandra says to me.

I shrug. 'Sure. Why not. It's a good cause.'

And, sadly, the scenery change actually *is* welcome.

'Stephanie?'

The latest addition to the flats looks up from her notebook. 'No, thanks. I just want to stay here.'

'How's Leo doing?'

She shrugs. 'No change.'

Stephanie's baby is the only one in the NICU who was born at full-term. Ben says he looks huge, but I think our perspectives are just skewed. He has something wrong with his heart, but no one seems entirely sure what.

'Sometimes it's like that. Something will happen soon,' Cassandra says.

'Yeah,' Stephanie says, suddenly getting up and

grabbing her notebook. 'That's what I'm afraid of.'

Cassandra follows her out. She and Stephanie seem to have really hit it off. Gwen and I return to eating and wonder what they'll be saying.

I can't believe I'm doing this. I'm sitting, with a dozen other women, in the middle of a shopping centre, with my air horns on and people literally watching my every move. Well, my nipples' every move. I did try to put on a scarf to cover the horns, but Gwen insisted it defeated the object. I did point out that the other mothers had their babies to cover their nipples, but she wouldn't have it. I've already had a toddler wander over and be completely fascinated. Then she was taken away by her father, who I strongly suspect felt the same.

Please don't let anyone I know be shopping here today.

Gwen is blatantly loving it, although I suspect her enthusiasm has less to do with the cause and more with feeding an exhibitionist streak. She's appointed herself border guard and has been prowling around - while pumping - in case anyone dares to make a rude comment. She's now cornered a pregnant woman and is showing her in detail how the pump works. By which I mean, she has the woman's face about an inch from her boobs. Judging by the woman's expression, she hasn't made a convert.

'Jessica? What in the world are you doing?'

I feel cold dread as I look up and find myself facing Amelia. 'It's a nurse-in,' I say, trying to pretend I feel I belong. 'I'm standing up for the rights of babies to eat when they need to.'

'But you're not even breastfeeding,' Amelia says, re-draping six thousand shopping bags over her arms.

'I am. Just with the help of an intermediary,' I say, quoting Gwen. 'Anyway, you must have loads of shopping to do...'

'Yes, I should be going and you should be coming with me,' Amelia says. 'You can't stay here making such a spectacle of yourself. What if someone I know sees you? What will they think?'

Gwen magically appears by my shoulder. 'Need help, Jess?'

Amelia visibly stiffens.

I think about it. 'No,' I say after a minute. 'I've got it. I'm staying, Amelia. I don't care what your friends think, or even what you think. I'm not doing anything wrong and I'm helping to support an important cause. You're entitled to your own opinion, but for once in your life just keep it to yourself. Goodbye.'

Amelia looks stunned. 'Well... okay,' she says, after a minute. 'We'll just... talk about it later.'

'Feel good?' Gwen asks as she walks off.

'Oh, yeah.'

It's amazing how easy that was. Suddenly I feel better about this whole thing.

'Hey, everyone!' Gwen calls. 'I think we should sing!'

Then again.

Ben sticks his head round the door of the common room that evening. 'I've got rid of the bike.'

'What?'

'Got myself a car, complete with car seat. Want to see?'

He leads me out to the car park and to his car. I can't quite believe what I'm seeing.

'You can't drive around in that.'

'Whyever not?'

'It's a girl's car.'

Specifically, it's a powder blue Nissan Micra.

Ben sighs. 'There's the bubble again. It's a car, Jess. Low mileage, full service history.'

'You can't tell me the guy who sold it to you didn't find it funny?'

Ben cracks his knuckles. 'Well, maybe he did. But that's his problem. This was the best car I could get with the money I've got. And I have to have something to carry Edward round in. I couldn't very well strap him to the back of the bike.'

'Edward's really doing well, then?'

'Much, much better. Fixing that heart thingy made a massive difference. He's still on CPAP, but they've actually tried him on just oxygen a few times and he's coped pretty well. Hopefully he'll be off that soon too.'

'That's wonderful.'

He grins. 'Yeah. Hence why I actually bit the bullet and sold the bike. Got to prepare for my new life as a dad.'

I eye the car again, but keep my mouth shut about it. 'Have you talked to his mother?'

A shadow passes across Ben's face. 'No. I email her progress reports, but... I don't know. I just can't bring myself to talk to her right now. She's been in to visit, apparently. Which is good, I guess. Though maybe it was just guilt.'

'Maybe.' I toe the ground.

'I wanted to ask your opinion on something. Do you think there's enough room in the back for two adults?'

I look. 'Debatable.'

'Only one way to find out, I suppose.'

For the record: there is, so long as you don't mind getting friendly.

Chapter 16

Samantha is now nine weeks old and 5lb 3oz. She's had a repeat eye test - no change. The physio is full of cold, so can't come this week. Yesterday she had her second ever bath. She seemed to like being in the water much more than last time. She didn't even poop.

My nipple looks damaged again. I keep smothering it with cream, and I've taken to bathing it in an eggcup of salt water to try to speed the healing, but it's still persisting. And pumping is really starting to hurt.

I'm finishing yet another session, when I take a look at my bottles and am horrified to see that the milk in one is pink. And I mean candy floss.

'Gwen!' I shriek.

Two minutes later, Gwen and Cassandra have wheeled their pumps through, and we're all sitting round staring at my breasts. We seem to spend a worrying amount of time either looking at them or discussing them. And to think I used to be too embarrassed to have a bra fitting.

'I think you might have a nipple infection,' Gwen says. 'How long has it been like that?'

'A few days.'

'How does pumping feel?'

'Sort of... agony.'

'Sounds like more antibiotics for you.'

My shoulders slump.

'And you need to get the doctor to swab your nipple and see if it's thrush, because if it is you'll have to chuck the milk from that breast.'

I have to forcibly restrain myself from hurling the pump across the room.

'That's it!' I yell, tears pricking my eyes. 'I've had it. I must have had every problem going. I had to take drugs to make enough milk, and now I do it's just one agonising infection after another! At this rate, by the time Samantha's a year old there won't be a single antibiotic she hasn't had. So much for boosting her immune system! What am I supposed to do if she actually gets sick? Invent another one?'

'You have had some rotten luck,' Gwen says sympathetically.

'Maybe I should just quit,' I say despondently. 'I'm obviously not cut out for this. If it weren't for the miracle of medical science, I wouldn't even be making milk.'

'If it weren't for the miracle of medical science, all our babies would be dead,' Cassandra says.

We both turn to look at her.

'I'm sorry,' she chokes out. 'I don't know why I said that.'

She dissolves into tears. I join her. Gwen digs in her bag and produces a large bar of chocolate.

It's a moment of ambivalence. I'm upset and crying, but at the same time I feel the warmth that comes from going through this with others instead of on my own.

So I go to the doctor. Again. And I get antibiotics. Again. And I get swabbed for thrush. When the doctor calls to confirm that's what I have, I nearly break down. Then I go and throw out everything I've made in the past few days - except the most recent stuff from the non-infected breast, which Gwen wisely told me to label - and cry.

In a few days, the agonising pain while pumping subsides. I'm briefly grateful. Until I realise that the physical pain had been keeping the emotional pain at bay.

I sit pumping, yet again. It's a bad session. One where I'm desperate to rip the horns off my chest and smash the pump against the wall. Even one more second feels unbearable.

I hear the sound of someone coming in. 'Gwen?'

'That's me.'

'Can you come in here a minute?'

'What's on your mind?' Gwen asks, when she comes into my cubicle.

'I'm thinking about stopping pumping,' I confess, through gritted teeth. 'Breastfeeding, as well. I really hate it.'

'What are we talking about here? Pain?'

'No, it's...' I struggle to find the words. 'It makes me feel bad. Like... angry sometimes, sad sometimes. Just... bad. I've... Well, I've never really liked having my nipples played with, and I thought it would be different when I was feeding a baby, but it just isn't. I spend our feeds just wanting to rip her off me. I feel the same about the pump. To be honest, even the thought of carrying on until she's a year corrected makes me want to stab myself.'

Gwen pauses. 'What do you want here? Do you want me to encourage you to carry on? Or support you in quitting? Because I can do both.'

'I was looking for your honest opinion of what I should do.'

'Quit.'

'Really?' I ask. 'Aren't you a breastfeeding supporter?'

'I am, but I am a greater supporter of women's sanity. You have to balance the benefits to the baby with the impact on the mother. It's like with these women you hear about every now and then, who had major postnatal depression, refused to take drugs in case they got into the milk, and then ended up throwing themselves off a bridge. If you feel like you said you feel, I reckon carrying on is going to do more harm than good in the long run.'

I feel choked up. 'Thanks,' I say, wiping away a tear. 'I didn't think anyone would understand.'

'I don't know if I do, really. It's not something I went through. But I've come across it before. It's called sad nipple syndrome.'

I stare at her. 'It has a name?'

'Yeah. There's not a lot out there about it, although there's a bit more about something called D-MER which is similar. You're not the only one, not by a long shot.'

I can't help it. I actually start to cry.

'Ah, don't worry,' Gwen says, hugging me as I sob. 'There's a hell of a lot of mothers out there. The one thing you can always be sure of: if you're going through it, someone else has too.'

I almost laugh at that. When you think about it, it's pretty arrogant to think that you're unique among all the billions of mothers throughout history.

'But don't just stop. You'll have to cut down slowly, or you're pretty much guaranteed another dose of mastitis.'

I grimace. 'Consider me warned.' I sigh. 'I just... I feel

guilty.'

'Of course you do. Guilt is the natural state of motherhood and everyone feels guilty about something they do or don't do.'

That doesn't make me feel better. No one ever mentioned *that* to me before I got pregnant. Surely constant guilt isn't a healthy way to live?

I carry on pumping as normal that day, feelings swirling around in my brain. It's not that I don't know what I want to do, I just don't know if I should do it. I've no idea where to find the balance between my needs and Samantha's. Are my emotional needs more important than her physical ones? Exactly how much difference does breastfeeding make? I google it and find so much conflicting information. Some people talk like formula feeding is akin to neglect; others claim it makes no difference. I don't know.

By morning, I've reached at least a temporary decision. I'm going to push on until Samantha comes out of hospital. I'm too afraid of the dangers of infection to stop before then. If a super bug got in and harmed Samantha, I just don't think I could live with myself. I've made it this far, so I must be able to do that much. Just knowing that I'm not crazy and not unique helps some. When she gets home, I'll try her on formula and start cutting down. I think if I could go down to part-time pumping, I might be able to carry on a little longer. It's going to be a feat of endurance, but Samantha's had to bear worse in her short life. I'd better prove to her that Mummy is tough too.

A few days later, Gwen comes into the common room with a weird look on her face.

'What's the matter?' Cassandra asks.

Gwen stops before the table and takes a deep breath. 'Ianto... they're discharging him. We're going home.'

A lump appears in my throat. Cassandra looks ready to cry.

'Oh... that's wonderful,' I say, putting as much enthusiasm as I can into my voice. 'Congratulations.'

'Yes... congratulations.'

Gwen looks between us with a wry smile. 'Flipping hell. Anyone would think you were going to miss me.'

Cassandra bursts into tears. I feel them pricking my eyes too. Miss her? I honestly don't know how I'll manage without her.

I run to her and hug her tightly.

'When do you go?' Cassandra asks, approaching us awkwardly and wiping her eyes.

'Gareth is taking the day after tomorrow off and driving up. We'll be heading out sometime in the afternoon.'

'That soon?'

Gwen shrugs. 'You know what they're like here about giving notice. To be honest, I knew he was getting close. I just didn't want to tempt fate by saying anything.'

I pull Cassandra into a three way hug. 'We'll miss you,' I say, I hope unnecessarily. 'I don't know what I would have done without you.'

'I do my best, chick,' Gwen says, wiping away a tear of her own. 'I've been thinking maybe I should write a book. *What to Expect When You're No Longer Expecting,* or something like that. Or maybe become a health visitor, or a breastfeeding supporter or something. When Ianto's a bit older.'

'Do it,' I tell her, trying to smile.

Cassandra starts to cry again. 'How am I supposed to go on without you?'

Gwen releases me to hug her properly. 'Ah chick, you'll manage. And I'll only be a phone call away.'

Cassandra nods. She doesn't look convinced.

When I push my way through the door to the flats that evening, the door to Stephanie's room is standing open. All her things are gone.

'She left,' Cassandra says from the lounge. 'Packed up and went. You just missed her.'

I go through. She's sitting at the table, an uneaten chicken curry in front of her, looking blankly at the TV.

'But Leo?'

'He didn't make it.'

'What?' I sit limply down in the chair next to her.

'Whatever's wrong with his heart just wasn't fixable. He started going rapidly downhill last night. They decided to take him off life support this morning.'

'Oh, my goodness.'

My stomach is clenched. I want to run to Samantha, gather her up in my arms, hold her tight and never let her go.

'Lucky her,' Cassandra says, stabbing a piece of chicken.

I stare at her. 'Lucky! How is she lucky?

'At least it's over for her. She can go home.'

I stare at her in disbelief. 'Her baby is dead and you think she's lucky because she can sleep in her own bed again? What are you thinking, Cassandra?'

Cassandra puts her head in her hands. 'You don't understand. Your baby's doing fine. In a few weeks, you'll take her home and it'll be like nothing has happened. You have no clue what it's like sitting here waiting for your baby to die.'

'What are you talking about?' I say, sitting down next to her. 'Tom's okay.'

Out of nowhere, she's hysterical. 'He isn't! He isn't! He's going to die. I know he's going to die!'

'Cassandra, listen to me,' I say, grabbing her by the shoulders and trying not to panic. 'Tom is fine. He's growing; he's healthy. It's going to be okay.'

'He's not!' Cassandra grabs a cushion from the sofa and starts yanking bits of thread off it. 'Why won't everyone stop pretending and tell the bloody truth? Everyone knows the boys do worse than the girls. I knew it was hopeless from the start. Why can't he just die and let it end?'

She dissolves into sobs. I sit down beside her. I try to put my arm around her, but she shies away, hugging the pillow to her chest.

'I really don't think it works like that.'

She looks up. 'All my life,' she says, 'I've been haunted by this. That I'm too lucky. That something terrible is out there for me, and it just hasn't caught up with me yet. And when I went into labour so early, I was sure the day had finally come. But it still hasn't. I can't take the waiting anymore.'

I sit there, feeling helpless. Knowing that I don't know what to do.

'I think you need to see a counsellor.'

She turns to look at me. 'What's the point?' she asks. 'I don't need anyone to tell me I've gone bonkers. If it weren't for the anti-depressants, I'd have thrown myself under a train long since. I'd do it now if I knew where the station was.'

I stare at her for a few seconds. What do I say? What do I do? I'm sure I'm supposed to stay with her, but then how do I get help?

I grab my phone. Gwen doesn't answer. Ben's goes straight to voicemail. In desperation, I call the NICU.

'I know how hard it can be,' Gwen says. 'And I know the doctors won't say it in case something goes wrong, but the reality is that the premature babies who don't go home are the exception. If they're born healthy, the care and the technology are there to pull them through.'

The three of us are crammed onto Gwen's bed in a three way cuddle, with Gwen in the middle. It's the kind of set up that a woman understands and a man mentally undresses.

'I know that,' Cassandra says after a minute. 'I'm just scared to accept it. Just in case mine is the exception. Stephanie's baby was.'

'Stephanie's baby wasn't healthy. He wasn't here because he was early. Sometimes they don't grow right, and there's nothing that can be done.'

'And those poor babies in Cardiff.'

Gwen takes a deep, shuddering breath. 'I've no answer to that one. That just wasn't fair. But bad things happen all the time. You can't live convinced that they're about to happen to you, or you'd never get out of bed.'

'I vote we don't,' Cassandra murmurs. 'I think we should just stay here and sleep.'

Gwen kisses her on the forehead. 'That's the postnatal depression talking. Give it a couple of weeks and the new dosage should have got you back on an even keel. Then things will only look miserable instead of hopeless!'

I laugh against her shoulder. 'I can't believe this is my life.'

'I can't believe I'm on drugs,' Cassandra mumbles.

Gwen looks between us. 'I can't believe this is the closest I've been in ten years to a threesome.'

It's funny. When I came here, a joke like that would have had me jumping off the bed. Now I even manage a smile.

'Oh, shut up, Gwen,' Cassandra says fondly. 'The only one here Jess and I might have a threesome with is Ben.'

'Mmmm,' I agree.

'And between you and me,' Cassandra says. 'He's quite good.'

I go rigid.

'What?' Gwen asks.

'Nothing,' I say, trying to relax again. 'Just thought I heard a noise.'

I can feel Gwen looking at me, but I avoid her gaze.

Later that evening, I hear Ben's door close and know he's back. I haul myself off the bed and go knock on it.

'Hey, Jess. Good day?'

'Up and down. Gwen's leaving.'

'She said.' Ben steps back and moves into the room. 'First graduate of our group.'

'Yes. It's wonderful.'

I stay in the doorway.

'Something on your mind?'

'You slept with Cassandra.'

Ben nods. 'Yeah, why?'

I feel wrong-footed. I was expecting... I don't know. Denial? Guilt? Regret? Some sort of reaction?

'Why?'

He shrugs. 'Stress relief, comfort. You know what it's like in this place.'

'Yes, but...'

'What?'

'She's married. Doesn't that bother you?'

'She's the one who's made promises, not me. And it was her idea.'

'Haven't you learnt your lesson about casual sex?'

'Of course. I used a condom.'

'That's not what I meant.' I tug at my shirt. 'I don't understand you.'

'No,' he says, wryly. 'I don't really understand you either.'

'I thought we had something. Or might have.'

'We do. We're friends.'

'No. A... special something.'

Ben looks taken aback. 'But you're engaged.'

'I know, but...'

'But?'

I can feel everything rapidly slipping away from me. 'Well... I told you I wasn't sure I wanted to get married after all.'

Ben lets out a slow breath. 'I was just taking that as stress talking.'

'Oh.'

He cracks his knuckles. 'Look... I thought you were just looking for a friend,' he says, no apparent malice in his tone. 'We're all trapped in this little bubble now - and it's intense - but soon we're going to go home and back to real life. I'll have enough on my plate working and taking care of Edward without starting a new relationship. I don't even know if I want anything serious yet. And your baby's father is still around, and he sounds like a decent guy, so why would you chuck that away when you've just had a baby?'

I find myself thinking of Ryan. He's far from perfect, but when it comes down to it, he's a good bloke. And he's Samantha's father. And the truth is... I do love him.

I think I've let the bubble get into my head.

'You're right,' I say, suddenly wanting to get away. 'This isn't real life. I think I forgot for a while. No hard feelings. See you around.'

And I hurry off to the pumping room - because it's the one place I can guarantee that he won't go.

I find my mind drifting back to the day Ryan proposed. Normally, when he tries to be romantic things don't quite work out - as with our candle-lit dinner a few weeks back - but that once it did.

We hiked up Gunnerside Gill, which is a fair trek up a steep river valley. It was February last year. There was no snow, but the trees were white with frost and walking through the woods got us singing 'Walking in a Winter Wonderland'. When we reached the top, where the waterfall is, Ryan produced a cushion from the over large backpack I'd been teasing him about, so I didn't have to sit on the cold stone. We sat together and shared a Mars bar, talking about the future. Then he took my gloved hand, said a lot of things I'd never thought would pass his lips without some form of torture being involved, went down on one knee and pulled out a ring box. He didn't even kneel in a cow pat or drop the box in the river. And he asked. And I said yes. Because I knew I wanted to be with him.

I don't know what's happened to my head these last few months. Thinking over what I know of Ben, I can't even see now why I thought we would work. He's not *bad*, he just... has a different value system. And maybe some of it I could stand to adopt, but some of it... I couldn't.

I sit and cry over what an idiot I've been.

Chapter 17

Gwen is on the phone when I get into the common room, speaking in a language I don't understand. It's bizarre, like I'm dreaming.

'Was that Welsh?' I ask, when she hangs up.

'Yup.'

'I didn't think anyone actually spoke Welsh.'

She grins. 'Let me guess: *Gavin & Stacey*?'

I smile sheepishly. 'Yeah.'

'Most don't, but some do, especially out in the country. That was my mother-in-law. She lives deep in the hills and she... well, she *must* be able to speak English, but she refuses to. First time I met her was ridiculous. You had me on one side, her on the other and Gareth in the middle translating. So, I decided I had to learn.'

'Was it hard?'

Gwen rolls her eyes. 'You have no idea. Welsh is just the ultimate bitch language. One of those where you use one word on weekdays, another on weekends, a third in February and a fourth if there's a full moon. Listen to Rhod Gilbert rant about it; he puts it best. And now I *can* speak it, she just calls and complains at me more often. So why I bothered I don't know. Anyway, what's occurring?'

'Nothing.'

'Anything on your mind?' She gives me a meaningful

look.

I sigh. I fill her in on Ben. 'Was this some weird coping mechanism? Creating some silly fantasy to take my mind off things? Making me pull away from Ryan just when we should have been pulling together?'

'Sounds like it,' Gwen says. 'It's this place: it's a marathon. And none of us trained for it, so we just fall down and struggle to pick ourselves back up. Sleep-deprivation, hormones and stress turn us all a bit bonkers, and people react in all sorts of strange ways. If I'd told anyone some of what went through my head the first time around, they'd have locked me up. We all have our coping mechanisms. Some people eat. Pretty sure some drink – though hopefully not the pumpers. Some people get obsessed with how much milk they're making or how much weight they've lost. And I run around trying to convince all the other mums that life isn't so terrible, in a futile effort to convince myself. Let's face it, you're just one of a bunch.'

That makes me feel a little better.

'Should I tell Ryan?'

'Dunno. What do you think?'

'I don't know!' I say, throwing up my hands. 'That's why I'm asking you.'

'Well, I don't know him. I only know you to a limited extent. You haven't actually done anything with Ben. My husband and I have an honesty policy about these things, but it depends on what impact you think telling him will have. Will he hold it against you?'

'I don't think so,' I say. 'He's not vindictive and he doesn't hold grudges. If he did, he wouldn't have any friends left, the things those boys have done to each other over the years. I think he'd tell me he forgave me and then never talk about it again.'

'Doesn't sound like a bad kind of guy to have.'

'No.' I fiddle with my engagement ring. 'You know the worst thing? Ryan's always seemed to think that I'm too good for him.'

'Best way for it to be,' Gwen says. 'Men only get down on one knee when they're convinced that they've made the catch of their life, and the only way they're going to hold onto it is to marry them before they realise.'

'Yes, but I thought so too,' I confess, hating myself. 'And I don't even know why, really. I guess because my dad said so. But... I think he was just being a dad.'

'Most likely.'

'I think that's why we didn't just get married when I found out I was pregnant. A part of me thought something better was out there for me. More exciting. But I think I've finally realised what a load of nonsense that is. I've got a good man - not perfect, but good - who loves me and who I love. And I should have grabbed him before he had the chance to realise how much better he could do.'

Gwen pushes back her curls. 'Look, any long-term relationship has got to be able to weather the times when one or both of you is acting like an arse. You've been through a bad patch, but it's made you realise how much you really love him, so go tell him that and apologise for being a mardy cow.'

'Should I go on my knees?' I joke.

'Might help,' Gwen says. 'Depends what you do while you're down there.'

I'm thinking in my room when Laura calls me to find out how Samantha is doing.

'I saw Ryan in Tesco,' she says, when I've updated her. 'He's really slimmed down, hasn't he? He must be the only one of us who's actually kept their New Year's resolution. I might have to ask him for tips.'

I dimly remember Ryan announcing he was going to lose his extra pounds. And me saying, 'Yes, dear' and not believing a word of it. I've noticed no change. I get another sharp stab of guilt.

'Bet he's been complaining about me a lot,' I say. 'Staying up at the hospital all the time.'

'Not that I've heard. In fact, Cracker was saying...'

Cracker is Laura's brother.

'... that Perky was making noise about you not being around for Ryan's birthday and stuff, and Ryan had a right go at him.'

More guilt. 'Really?'

'Yeah. Went on about how his daughter needed her mother and how you were so incredible giving up everything to look after her.'

And this after all I've said about him over the last few months. I feel like crying again.

'He's good like that,' I say. 'Loyal to a fault.' It's just another thing I've forgotten lately.

'Yeah.'

There's a short silence.

'Jess?'

'What?'

'Well... you know when you came home for that visit, and we all came round?'

'Yes.'

'You remember what you were talking about?'

Frankly, no. I barely remember this morning.

'About... your friend in the NICU and what she said about you... knowing people.'

Huh?

'You know, how you probably knew people, but didn't know because they hadn't told you?'

'Sorry, Laura,' I say, yawning. 'I've got raging baby brain. You'll have to spell it out.'

Silence, then, 'About how you might have a friend who was gay.'

Oh, right.

Oh... *right*.

'So, you're saying you're...'

'Yes.'

'Since when?'

'Since always.'

'But you went out with that guy, Jamie, for ages. And you said you split up because he moved away.'

'Yes. He lives in Brighton now. He runs a beauty parlour.'

I hesitate. 'I'm trying not to pay so much attention to stereotypes.'

'In this case, the stereotype is dead on.'

'Oh.'

'Yeah.'

'But... that seemed to work well.'

'It did. We were mates. But I want more than that now.'

I rub my hand over the duvet cover. 'So... you're telling everyone?'

A pause. 'Well, some people already know.'

'Who?'

'Well, my parents and Cracker, obviously. And some of the rest of my family. And... the girls.'

'Which ones.'

'Well... all of them.'

'Oh.' I clench the duvet cover in my fist. 'When did you tell them?'

Laura sighs. 'A while ago.'

I feel slighted, but then I feel ashamed.

'I think I know why you didn't tell me,' I say finally. 'I've been a bit... narrow-minded, I suppose. I'm trying to do better, but I just... How do you expand your mind?'

'Exposure to different ways of life, I suppose. Travel, study, meeting different people.'

I smile wryly. 'I think I should have done this before having a baby.'

'You still can. Just not in quite the same way.'

I wonder if there's such a thing as a mind-widening course. Maybe I should ask Gwen to devise me one. That is, if she hasn't already.

'Anyway,' Laura says, 'I wanted to ask if you could put me in touch with that friend of yours who you were talking about.'

'Gwen?' I hesitate. 'She's actually married.'

I can almost hear Laura rolling her eyes. 'I didn't mean for a date. I just thought it would be good to talk to someone who understands. If you think she wouldn't mind.'

I laugh. 'She won't mind. She *will* make it her mission to get you out and proud.'

'That would probably help too.'

'I'll remind you that you said that,' I say. 'So... are you

telling everyone else?'

'Actually, I'm thinking of moving away.'

'No!' I grip the covers tightly. 'You don't have to do that. I mean... everyone will be okay with it.'

There's a few moments' silence.

'It's not that,' she says. 'It's just... I'll always be unusual here. And some people can handle that. Hell, some even like it. But I'm not one of them. I don't want to be different. I mean, I want to be honest about who I am, but I just... want it to be no big deal. And if I move somewhere larger — somewhere that actually has a gay community — I can fit in at least some of the time. Can you understand that?'

I stare at the wall opposite. I remember sitting round with the girls, feeling left out and different and hating it. 'Yes, I think I can. It's just... I don't want you to go. And I hate that you feel you need to, just to be you.'

'Me too.'

It's times like this that I think Gwen and the others are right, and the world I live in isn't such a wonderful place after all.

We wave Gwen off on a cold Thursday afternoon. Ianto looks in danger of disappearing into the depths of his car seat, and he's buried under blankets and a woolly hat.

'Drive safely,' I tell Gwen, trying not to start crying again. Beside me, Cassandra nods in agreement, lips pressed tightly together.

'We will,' Gwen says, hugging both of us. 'And you two just keep on going. It shouldn't be long now. This *is* going to end.'

I guess it is, but I can't believe it. It feels like this time will go on forever.

When she's gone, Cassandra and I sit together on her bed feeling morose and her absence.

'How are you doing?' I ask awkwardly.

'I'm stable. Doctor upped my dose, but it'll take a couple of weeks to know if it's working.'

'Are you going to be okay in the meantime?'

She turns her head away. 'It's not that bad usually. Just with Stephanie leaving, on top of a bad day. I went to pieces. Sorry for freaking you out.'

'Sorry I got freaked out.'

'I thought you coped quite well.'

We sit in silence.

'I wish Gwen was still here,' Cassandra says. 'Even if she *has* been driving me nuts. She's had me on suicide watch and wouldn't leave me alone. Even slept on my floor. And she snores.'

I snort.

'Honestly. It's horrendous. Sounds like a dodgy vacuum cleaner.'

More silence.

'Do you want me to sleep on your floor tonight?' I ask.

'Kind of.'

'Okay then.'

I fiddle with the duvet cover. 'Where do you live, anyway?' I ask. 'I don't think I ever found out.'

'Richmond.'

'Oh, really?' We're not that far apart then.' I feel stupidly awkward. 'We could get together once we get home. Have playdates and stuff.'

'Yeah,' Cassandra says, giving me a smile. 'We could do that.'

Maybe I don't need to find a whole new set of friends after all.

'Cassandra,' I ask slowly. 'You and Ben...'

She snorts. 'There's no me and Ben. It was... I don't know what it was. A bit of comfort, I suppose. It was stupid.'

'Are you going to tell your husband?'

'Already did.' She smiles wryly. 'The truth is, he cheated on me while I was pregnant so he can't really complain. Ironically, I think it's actually improved things between us. Made us feel equal again. Guess sometimes two wrongs do make a right.'

I stretch out my legs. 'How did life get so messed up?'

'I don't know,' she says. 'I really don't.'

And we sit there until the clock tells us we need to pump again.

Chapter 18

Samantha is now 10 weeks old and weighs 5lb 10.5oz. She is on her last package of size 0 nappies and will soon be in newborn size. They're a bit big, but she'll probably grow out of them before we know it. She's slowly taking more and more milk from the bottle and less and less from the feeding tube. I can't wait for it to come out.

Friday night, with Cassandra much improved and safely at home for the weekend, I decide to call Ryan to pick me up. I've called him every night since I spoke to Ben and tried to "reconnect" as the relationship experts say. I can feel the distance between us, though, even down the telephone line. When I stop to think about it, I feel a cold dread that the last few months have done irreparable damage to our relationship. So much for children bringing you closer together.

I trudge wearily through the door of Mum's house, Ryan following behind me. I trail through to the kitchen and stop short. Ryan nearly ploughs into the back of me.

Mum is sitting at the table with Brian Blessed Howard, in the middle of tea. Mum is wiping gravy off his beard. There's nothing to it, and yet it seems shockingly intimate.

'Mum.'

Mum jumps a little and drops the napkin. 'Jess! I

wasn't expecting you back tonight.'

Obviously.

'Yeah... it was a spur of the moment thing,' I say. 'Sorry to interrupt.'

'Don't be silly,' Mum says hurriedly, getting up to give me a hug. 'You're not interrupting. This is your home.'

Maybe it is, but it feels less and less like it.

'Hi, Howard,' I say awkwardly. 'Nice to meet you properly.'

He gives me a smile and gets to his feet. He's quite a large man. Not I'm-trapped-in-my-house large, just... barrel chested I think is the term. And tall. Not much like my dad.

'Hi, Jess,' he says warmly. 'And Ryan, is it?'

Ryan moves round me to shake Howard's hand. 'Nice to meet you, sir.'

Brown-noser.

'Are you joining us?' Howard asks, gesturing to the table. 'Mary made more than enough for four. I think she's trying to fatten me up.' He laughs heartily at that. I manage a smile.

I'm sorely tempted to refuse and go hide upstairs, but my stomach rumbles in protest at that idea.

'Thanks,' I say. 'That would be wonderful.'

'I'll have to run off,' Ryan says. 'I didn't know you'd be home tonight, so I made plans.'

I feel a stab of envy that he can go out and not worry. Then I feel a stab of guilt to balance it out.

'Will you come round after that?'

He looks surprised. 'I can do. If that's fine with you, Mrs J?'

Ryan doesn't usually stay here with me; I go to his. To

allow Mum to pretend she's not condoning pre-marital sex.

Mind you, that may now be hypocritical of her.

I wish I hadn't thought that.

'I'm sure it will be fine,' Mum says, avoiding my eyes. 'Jess really needs your support right now.'

Ryan gives me a quick kiss and heads out.

'Don't get too drunk!' I call after him, fighting the desire to grab him and pull him back.

'I won't!'

That leaves three of us in the kitchen. Ironically, Howard is the one who looks most at home.

'Congratulations on your baby, Jess,' Howard says, as I sit down and Mum gets me a plate of food. 'Mary showed me the pictures. She's beautiful.'

'Oh... thanks,' I say, looking curiously at him. Most people don't talk like she's a normal baby.

'And Samantha's a lovely name. Does she have a middle one yet?'

'Not yet. We're not sure what to pick. Ryan wanted Annabel, but then her initials would spell SAW.' I pull a face.

He pulls one back as Mum sits down. 'Maybe not.'

'I suppose Emma is also out?' Mum says regretfully, setting a plate before me and sitting back down.

'SEW is slightly better, but I think I'd rather avoid words.'

'Nothing beginning with O then?' Howard jokes.

'I think SOW borders on child abuse.'

We eat in companionable silence. And I'm surprised by just how companionable it is. I would never have thought I'd be comfortable sitting down to dinner with Mum's boyfriend. I still struggle with the idea of them together.

But he seems nice.

'So... um... how long have you been...' What do I call it? Dating just sounds wrong. 'Uh, seeing each other?'

Mum goes rather pink. 'Oh... a few months.'

'How many months?'

'Um... six.'

'Six?' I repeat. 'Six whole months and you didn't tell me?'

Mum and Howard exchange glances. 'Jess, I didn't know how you would react. And you had such a hard time while you were pregnant, I didn't want to risk upsetting you,' Mum says.

'I wouldn't have been upset.'

Actually, I probably would have been.

'Jess, I know it must be strange for you, seeing your mother with someone else,' Howard says, laying down his fork. 'Mary felt - that is, we both felt - that it would be best not to say anything until we'd had time to see if it might be serious.'

I look from one to the other. 'So... it *is* serious, then?'

Mum blushes. 'Well, it's still quite early, but... we think - that is, we *feel* - that it is.'

I look down at my plate. 'Well... that's wonderful.'

Suddenly, I feel a stab of longing for my dad. To have us all round this table, having dinner together. Amelia and I sniping at each other and being told off. Not as children, you understand, as teenagers. We used to get on well when we were kids. Then, suddenly, it all went wrong. That's puberty, I guess.

Dad's death was sort of a surprise and sort of not. He had terminal cancer, like a frightening number of people these days, and he was starting to go down hill. He was facing a long, hard slide to the end. And then he died in a car crash. Instantly. No pain. Everyone kept saying it was a blessing. And it was. But I'd still lost my dad.

'It's really wonderful,' I say. 'This is really nice, Mum. Is there more?'

When Howard has gone home, Mum and I sit together on the sofa while I pump. Strange how a few weeks ago I would have balked at doing this in front of her. Now I'm beyond caring. I think sleep deprivation has destroyed the modesty centre in my brain.

'So... Howard,' I say. 'He seems nice.'

'He *is* nice.'

A minute of silence.

'He's... not much like Dad.'

'No.'

Another minute.

'But you... feel the same way about him?'

Mum takes a deep breath. 'Jess, your dad and I were soul mates. No, I don't feel the same way about Howard, but I don't expect to. That sort of thing just doesn't happen twice in one lifetime. But I do love him, and I think we can be very happy together. And now Amelia is married - and you soon will be - I'd like to have someone to share the rest of my life with. Because your dad isn't coming back, and I still have - I hope - a lot of years left.'

The timer on my phone beeps and I turn off the pump. 'I know,' I say, trying to hide the tears that have sprung up from nowhere. 'It's good. Really. I'm happy for you. And I'm sure we'll be...' My voice trails off.

'Mum, is Howard going to come and live here?'

'Well...' Mum says shyly. 'Maybe, at some point. Or I'll

live with him. Or we might sell both places and buy something together. But not yet. Plenty of time for you to get married. Don't worry, we won't be kicking you out!'

I busy myself breaking down my pumping gear.

'Have you and Ryan discussed a date yet?'

'No, not yet,' I say. 'Maybe we'll talk about it tonight.'

Although, there are other things we should talk about first.

After Mum has gone to bed, Ryan comes in. Slightly merry, but not too drunk. He flops down beside me on the sofa and gives me a sloppy kiss.

'I love you,' he says, nuzzling my neck.

I smile as the pump beeps and cuts off. 'Yeah, I know.'

I bring him a glass of water, and he drinks some of it while I clear up from pumping.

'Apparently, Cat Shagger...'

'I really wish you wouldn't call him that.'

'Fine, I'll use his name.' Ryan stops and scratches his head. 'What *is* his name?'

'Mervin.'

'Really? I think Cat Shagger's better.'

'No, it isn't.'

Just to reassure you, he didn't actually do what his nickname implies. The explanation is actually quite boring and involves a pencil sharpener.

Ryan brings his glass through to the kitchen. 'Fine. Apparently *Mervin* is seeing that girl who works on the checkout down the Coop.'

'Which one?'

'The one with the nose thingy.'

I pull a face. 'Well, each to their own.'

Then I chastise myself. She's probably very nice. Must do better.

He puts his arms around me. 'And Marbles has finally popped the question.'

'You're kidding?' I turn to stare at him. '*Marbles?*'

'I know. I owe Tenner... well, a tenner.'

Ryan packs up the steriliser as I wash things. 'And apparently they're thinking of tying the knot in the summer.'

'*This* summer?'

'Yeah.'

'Wow.'

'I know,' Ryan says. 'Never thought he'd go before me.'

I avoid his gaze. 'Well... maybe we could do it in the summer too.'

Ryan starts. 'Really?'

'Yeah. Because I was thinking... I've actually lost quite a bit of weight, and I suppose my stomach isn't really that bad and I can just get some control underwear or something and...'

I'm cut off when Ryan suddenly picks me up and twirls me round. It's very romantic for a second, until I thump my leg against the fridge.

'Ow!'

'Shit! Sorry.'

'It's okay,' I say, rubbing my leg when he puts me down. 'Just... you know... if you still want to? I know I haven't been much fun.'

Ryan shuffles his feet. 'Yeah... about that. I haven't been that much help either. I should have been around more. I... Look, don't tell anyone I said this, but... hospitals scare me shitless. And seeing her like she was in the early days... I couldn't handle it. I just wanted to run away.'

'I know the feeling.'

'Yeah, but you haven't run,' Ryan says, grabbing my hands. 'You've stayed there - *lived* there - given up your whole life, basically, to be there for her, and it's just amazing. I'm so bloody proud of you. Hell, I'm in *awe* of you. You're so incredible, and all I've done is moan about you forgetting my birthday and stuff, when that's because you've been busy with something so much more important.'

I wipe away a tear. 'Stop it! I'm not amazing. I should have remembered those things. I've been such a complete mess and I've got everything wrong. I...'

He grabs me and pulls me into a kiss. And even though it's just in the kitchen, beside a sink full of washing up and some leftover food, it feels like the most romantic kiss in the whole world.

Afterwards, we look at each other. 'I still love you,' Ryan says awkwardly.

I suppress the urge to cry. 'I still love you.'

Because I do. I honestly do. Even though I've forgotten it - a lot - over the past few weeks.

'So we're fine then?'

'Yeah.'

Could that really be all it takes?

Ryan puts the steriliser back into the microwave.

'Let's go to bed,' I say.

I lie awake for hours after Ryan has collapsed. Then I pump. Then I lie awake some more.

'Mmm, morning,' Ryan murmurs into my arm, some

time later. 'Sleep well?'

'Yeah.'

'Fancy a snuggle?'

'Okay.'

We curl up together.

'You're so tense,' Ryan says, after a few minutes. 'What's wrong?'

I'm turned away from him, staring at the wall. 'I want to tell you something. Well, actually, I don't want to tell you, but I think I need to. Especially if we're going to get married.'

'Right,' Ryan says. 'Do you want to look at me, then?'

I start to cry. 'No.'

'Hey, hey,' he says, slowly turning me over. I bury my face in his chest instead. 'It can't be that bad.'

I mutter into his chest.

'What?'

'I'm not sure how to explain it,' I sniff, wiping my eyes. 'I feel like I've had an affair.'

Ryan stiffens beside me.

'I haven't,' I add hastily. 'I mean, there was nothing physical. Well, we cuddled, but I did that with Gwen and Cassandra too, so I don't think it really counts. But... I thought about him. Romantically, I mean. I imagined us being together.'

There's silence for a few seconds.

'That's it?'

I nod.

'Do you want to break up?'

'No!'

'Are you still thinking of him like that?'

'No.'

'Well, then.' Ryan tips my head up. 'It doesn't matter, does it?'

'No?' I ask hopefully.

'No.' Ryan actually cracks a smile. 'I mean, you have thoughts like that about Ryan Reynolds, don't you?'

I laugh. 'I suppose I do.'

'So, it doesn't matter.'

It's a cliché, but I feel like a huge weight has been lifted off me.

Yeah, it's okay. It's going to be okay.

Chapter 19

Samantha is now 11 weeks old and 5lb 13oz. Her weight gain has slowed again, because she's working very hard. The nurses say she's behaving more like a full-term baby now. This means being awake more, demanding cuddles and crying for non-obvious reasons. Given the volume she can now produce, I'm not overly worried about the state of her lungs.

'She's looking much better,' Amelia says, handing Samantha to Mum. 'Almost like a real baby.'

I roll my eyes, but hold my tongue.

'She's beautiful,' Mum says, wiping a tear from her eye.

Beautiful is still a bit of a stretch. I think they may have overdone the supplements, because she's looking decidedly chubby at the moment. She still has her nose tube for oxygen and the sticky patches on her face to keep it in place. And there's still something not-quite-right about her face. But it's certainly a big improvement on how she started.

'They've taken her feeding tube out,' I boast. 'She can eat everything normally now.'

'Still needs oxygen, though,' Amelia says.

Trust her to look on the downside.

'How long will that last?' Mum asks.

I shrug. 'I don't know. Apparently, some babies

actually go home on it.'

Amelia looks appalled. 'You can't take her out like that. What will people think?'

'How about that she's lucky to be alive?' I snap.

'Girls!' Mum says, very firmly for her. 'How about we cross that bridge if we come to it?'

'Why are you always so obsessed with what people will think?'

'Because it's important.'

'No, it's not,' I say impatiently. 'So I had a baby before I got married, Samantha's on oxygen and Mum has a boyfriend. Big deal. If people don't understand, that's their problem.'

There's a brief silence, during which I realise what I've just said and curse myself.

Amelia looks at Mum. 'A boyfriend? Who?'

Mum glances at me. I wish she looked angry, but she just looks disappointed. 'Howard from church.'

'Brian Blessed Howard?'

It's hard to suppress a smile at that. It's the first time in years we've been on the same wavelength.

'Yes,' Mum says stiffly.

'You can't go out with him. What will...'

'Oh, shut up Amelia,' I interrupt.

'No, I will not!'

'Photos!' I snap and she goes quiet.

'What?' Mum asks.

Amelia and I share a look. 'Nothing,' I say and she mumbles the same.

There's an awkward silence all round.

'I'm planning on stopping pumping,' I hear myself say.

Judging by the look on Amelia's face, you'd think I'd

announced I was planning to cut off Samantha's oxygen supply.

'You can't do that! What will she eat?'

Does she really need me to answer that? Obviously, I'm going to feed her on gravy.

'Formula, Amelia.'

'But you're doing so well,' Mum says.

I sigh. 'Mum, I'm not doing well. I have to take drugs to make enough milk for her. My nipples are constantly getting damaged, and I've already had mastitis and a nipple infection.'

'Yes, but breastfeeding is such a wonderful experience.'

If only.

'Mum, it's not a wonderful experience. It's... I don't like it.'

She pats my hand. 'Well, it takes a while to get the hang of it.'

'It's not that, Mum. It's pumping too. It... makes me feel bad. Sucking on my... you know.'

Two uncomprehending faces stare at me.

'I always quite enjoyed it, actually,' Mum says.

'Never mind. Forget I said anything.'

I should have known they wouldn't understand.

'But you can't...' Amelia starts.

'Just shut up!' I snap. Then I try to soften my voice. 'Just... please. I don't want to talk about it. Please.'

Mum and Amelia exchange looks.

'So, Amy,' Mum says, 'how's the new job going?'

I'm passing the door of the common room, when Ben's voice calls, 'Jess!'

I hesitate. To be honest, I've been avoiding him as

much as possible. Not because I'm still fantasising about him, but because every time I see him I feel like an idiot.

'Hi, Ben,' I say awkwardly, from the doorway. 'How's Edward?'

'He's good,' Ben says. 'Really good. That's what I wanted to tell you. He's on just oxygen now, so our local hospital can take him. We'll be going this afternoon. I've just been packing up.'

'That's wonderful,' I say sincerely. 'I hope he'll be ready to go home soon.'

Ben gives me a half smile. 'Think we'll see each other again?'

'Probably not.'

'No,' he says. 'That's what I thought you'd say.'

We look at each other.

'I still consider you a friend, you know,' he says.

'Me too,' I say. 'Me too.'

Chapter 20

Samantha is now 12 weeks old and weighs 6lb 2oz. She's taking 100ml at some feedings.

She has had her hearing checked, and her ears are just fine. She's also had her second set of vaccinations, which I thought she took quite well. Compared to her first weeks when her heel was getting pricked several times a day, a couple of shots probably doesn't seem like much.

This week she's been spending more and more time off oxygen. She's down to only having it at meals now (since it's harder for her to breathe when she's eating). Apparently, the extra tube in her heart has closed on its own, as we hoped it would as she approached her due date, and the difference it's made is amazing.

Samantha is sitting in her bouncy chair, with a blanket wrapped around her. It seems weird to see her without her nasal cannula. I have to keep reminding myself that she doesn't need extra oxygen anymore. She's been moved into the best room; the one that actually has a window. It's good to feel the sun.

'We're going to do a car seat test on her, so we need you to bring it in,' the nurse says.

'A what test?'

'Basically, we'll put Samantha in her car seat for the same length of time as your journey home and check that her blood oxygen level is stable. If it is, she's pretty much good to go.'

'Go?'

'Yes, go!' the nurse laughs. 'Go home. She's off the oxygen and her stats are just fine. After the test, we'll take her off the monitor altogether. Congratulations, she's fully baked!'

It's all very well for her, but after all these weeks the idea of actually taking her home with me seems ludicrous. I suppose most new mothers feel like that, but their babies weren't still on oxygen three days ago.

'But she's still so small...' I let my voice trail off.

'She'll grow. It'll probably be two to three years before she catches up fully, but she'll get there.'

'But...'

'We can do a trial run,' the nurse says sympathetically. 'You'll stay with her overnight here. You'll be on your own, but we'll be within yelling distance if you need us. We can do up to three nights if you need them. But, trust me, before then you'll be ready.'

I sincerely doubt that.

I go home the next day, mainly so I can sit in my room surrounded by baby stuff and try to imagine actually bringing Samantha here. It's going to be cramped. I may have gone overboard with the baby shopping. Some people won't consider buying anything until they have their 20 week scan. By then, I'd bought *everything*. All we could possibly need and a good few things we will probably never use. Like the reusable nappies. Honestly, what was I thinking?

It makes you wonder: did I know on some level that

she would come early? And does that mean there was actually something wrong that no one detected?

I find myself thinking of Ryan's flat with the spare room (well, cupboard) and suddenly it doesn't seem so crazy to take her there.

I eventually get up to go to the toilet. On the way back, I hear voices. And crying. Frowning, I creep downstairs to investigate.

Amelia is sitting at the kitchen table, sobbing. Really sobbing. I haven't seen her cry in years. It feels like I've stepped into some weird alternate universe.

Mum is sitting beside her, comforting her.

'What's the matter?' I ask.

Amelia's head jerks up. She instantly assumes her normal expression and tries to look as if nothing is wrong. It really doesn't work.

'Everything is fine,' she says stiffly. 'Never better.'

'Come on, Amelia,' I say, sitting down on her other side. 'You can't expect me to believe that.'

'You really think I'm going to tell you? Just so you can gloat?'

I shift uncomfortably. 'I don't have to gloat.'

'You can't expect me to believe that. You always gloat.'

'Well, that's because you're always such a bitch to me!'

'Girls!'

'Well, it's true,' I protest. 'You criticise and tell me how to live my life, and I'm just sick of it.'

'And you're a smug bitch who gets everything she wants.'

'Now, really, stop it!' Mum says sharply, and we turn to her in shock. 'I've had enough of this. You've been this way since you were teenagers, and you still haven't grown out of it. Why in the world did this even start?'

'No idea,' I say sullenly.

'Oh, you don't know.'

I frown at Amelia. 'No, I really don't.'

'Oh, come on!'

'Amy!' I say. 'I. Don't. Know. If I did something, I'm sorry and I'd really like to know what it was.'

She stares at me, apparently stunned into silence by my use of her short name. 'You really don't, do you?'

'No!'

She mutters something I can't catch.

'What?'

'Ryan.'

'What about him?'

She turns red and avoids my gaze. Realisation slowly dawns. 'You *like* Ryan?'

'When we were teenagers, not now. I can't think what I ever saw in him.' She pauses. 'And, I mean that in the nicest possible way.'

Right.

'And all this time you've been mad at me for what... stealing him?'

A nod.

'Because *he* asked *me* out, you know. And I had absolutely no idea you even knew he existed.'

'Even after I went on and on about him for weeks?'

I rake through my sleep deprivation-addled memory. I dimly remember her having a major crush on some guy and just yattering on about him until I got so sick of it, I...

'That was Ryan?'

'I told you his name as soon as I found it out. I know I did.'

I fiddle with my ring. 'Yeah... I may have stopped listening by then. In fact, I may have started wearing earplugs because you were so incredibly *annoying* that I wanted to strangle you.'

'Oh.'

We look at each other.

'That's really how it all started?' I ask. I can't believe it. All these years of fighting because she fancied Ryan?

'It sounds a bit stupid when you say it out loud,' Amelia grudgingly admits. 'But I really thought you knew and you did it on purpose. I really had it bad for him. And it was right after I found out...'

She stops suddenly and shoots a glance at Mum.

'What?' I ask.

No answer.

'What?!' I say again. 'Look, I know people have been keeping secrets from me because they don't think I'll understand, but I'm learning to be more open-minded. If nothing else, I need the practice! It can't be that big a deal.'

'I'm adopted,' says Amelia.

I stare at her for a few seconds, not quite sure what to say.

'Really?' I whisper.

'But you're not.'

'Oh.'

I feel all off-balance, like I've just got off a boat.

Mum takes my hand. 'Your Dad and I thought we couldn't have children. We adopted Amelia and then a few years later you turned up from nowhere. We decided - maybe wrongly - that we should keep it a secret so that you both felt equal. And you *are* equal - you were both

162

brought to us by God.'

'I found out by accident,' Amelia says. 'And I reacted badly. I'd always felt like you got most of the attention, but finding that out and then the thing with Ryan... Well, I started to hate you.'

Mum takes her hand as well. 'You were probably right about Jess getting more attention,' she says quietly. 'Although we didn't mean to, we couldn't help but be overwhelmed when we had her after all those years. And then she got very ill when she was a baby and we nearly lost her. I had her firmly tied to my apron strings after that.'

'I never knew that!' I say.

'You were far too young to remember. And it wasn't something any of us cared to think about.'

I try to grasp the concept of Amelia not being my natural sister and me nearly dying as a child. I can't. It just sounds like a story book.

There's a long silence.

'So, what's the matter?' I ask again. 'I promise I won't gloat. I swear on... Samantha's life.'

That gets her. She fiddles with the table cloth. 'Eric has left me.'

I stare at her. 'Pardon?'

'For his secretary. He wasn't even original about it.'

'Oh. Oh dear.'

'I'm going to be divorced for another woman. And you know the worst thing?'

'What?'

'I've spent all these years trying to maintain a perfect figure - at least partly for his benefit - and he's thrown me over for someone who looks like the Michelin Man.'

I try to suppress a snort of laughter, but it escapes anyway. Eric is the thinnest man alive. She better not fall asleep on him, because I don't rate his chances of survival.

'Oh, thanks!'

'No!' I say hastily. 'I'm not laughing at you. Just the image of Eric with...'

The corners of her lips twitch. 'I guess it's quite funny.'

'I always thought he was a bit of a prat.'

She sighs. 'Yes, he's a lot of a prat actually. In fact, I'd go as far as to say that I can live quite happily without him. It's just the humiliation. What will people think?'

'Amy' I say, grabbing both her shoulders. 'Fuck people.'

'Jess!' Mum says.

'Sorry, Mum,' I say, not breaking eye contact. 'But I mean it. We both care far too much about stuff that most people don't give a crap about anymore. People come in all sorts of variations. Real friends accept you for who you are and the rest just don't matter.'

She sighs. 'Maybe not to you, but I'm afraid they do to me.'

'Well, I think that's something you should work on,' I say, not unkindly. 'But, in the meantime, you've got me and Mum to stand by you. And Ryan's never thought much of Eric. And just avoid anyone who's mean about it. Plus, Eric's the one who's left. Just think, you can call him all sorts for abandoning you and then you can string out the divorce for years just to punish him.'

She snorts. 'I might just do that. Could be quite fun.'

'That's the spirit,' I say.

Mum looks a bit out of her depth and is obviously searching for the right thing to say. 'Cup of tea?'

'Yes, please,' we chorus.

We are so English.

Before Ryan comes to pick me up, and when Mum's safely out of earshot in the loo, I corner Amelia.

'So, these photos,' I say. 'And that holiday. What happened?'

'You swear you won't tell?'

'Yes.'

'On the same condition as before?'

'Absolutely.'

She sighs. 'It wasn't much, really. You know I was talked into going on a "last fling" by the girls and... well... I had one. With a waiter.'

'Really?' I ask, slightly impressed. I can't imagine her saying anything to a waiter beyond, 'This meal is cold, bring me another.'

'It wasn't much really. Just making out.' She clears her throat. 'And maybe a touch of heavy petting. It was just a pre-marital wobble.'

She gives a half-smile. 'I was completely paranoid about Eric finding out. He's always made such a big thing about being my one and only. I don't know why I bothered now. In fact, I'm quite tempted to get those photos off Gwen and email them to him, just for a laugh.'

I grin back. 'Tempting, but I wouldn't. I reckon you can get more out of playing the victim. Not that you aren't, you understand, but you may as well get what you can. Make him suffer.'

'Agreed.'

We look at each other again.

'Does this mean we're friends?' I ask hesitantly.

She thinks about that. 'Sisters. Well... sort of.'

'No, we're sisters,' I say firmly, suddenly sure. 'We always have been.'

She smiles properly. 'Okay, then.'

Once we get back to the hospital, Ryan and I sit by Samantha's bedside, watching her sleep. Night is falling outside. The sunset might actually be romantic, if it weren't over a car park.

'They're talking about her going home soon,' I say.

Ryan lets out a slow breath. 'Wow,' he says, fiddling with his watch. Then he chuckles. 'I feel like I want to say "so soon", but that's stupid.'

I grab his hand and smile. 'No, it isn't. They say "home" and it feels like we're totally unprepared. Even though yesterday it felt like we'd been here forever.'

'You think we're ready?'

'No.'

'Me neither.'

I squeeze his hand. 'Silly, really. I mean, we've... well, *I've* had nurses showing me how to do everything. Changing nappies, feeding, holding, bathing. Who gets that anymore? We've got to be better prepared than most first-time parents. And, after what we've been through the last few months, we must be up to looking after one small baby.'

'Yeah.'

We look at each other.

Ryan shifts in his seat. 'I might just call round to your mum's and check there's a lock on the sink cupboard. Just so she doesn't drink bleach, you know? I know she can't crawl yet, but... well, never too soon to get onto it, right?'

'Right.'

I try to imagine actually taking her home. Just putting her in the car seat and driving out of here and heading...

'Ryan,' I say, 'I don't want to take her home to my mum's. I want to take her home together.'

He looks at me, wonder on his face. 'I thought you were dead set against that until we got married? Remember that whole discussion? What about what people will think?'

'Yeah,' I say, pursing my lips. 'Maybe that doesn't matter as much as I thought it did. I mean, most of this country thinks it's normal to live together when you've got a kid, even if you're not married. And we're engaged. It's not like I got pregnant off a one night stand in a nightclub toilet.'

'Who did that?'

'Oh... no one. Just saying. Anyway.' I grin at him. 'Let's move in together.'

A huge grin spreads over his face. 'Yeah?'

'Yeah.'

He looks down again at our joined hands. 'Cool.'

We sit in silence, sneaking looks at each other.

'Oh, bugger,' he says suddenly.

'What?'

'I'm going to have to go round to your mum's and get all the baby stuff. What do I tell her? She'll probably chase me off with the carving knife!'

'Ryan!'

'I'll have to sneak in when she's not around. When does she go to church? I'll go then. I'll get Donkey round with the van. We should be able to clear everything while she's out.'

I have to laugh. 'It sounds like you're planning a break in. Don't tell me you're afraid of my mother?'

'Confidentially?'

'Yes.'

He leans over and whispers in my ear. 'I'm afraid of your mother.'

I kiss him. 'Don't worry. I'll call her. Maybe I'll go round.'

'Want me to come too?'

'No, it's okay.' I stub my toe into the floor. 'What I really need is Gwen. This is just the kind of thing she loves.'

'Have you spoken to her?'

'Yeah, once or twice.'

'But?'

I shrug. 'We're out of the bubble now. Back to reality. I'll try to stay in touch, but I don't think it's going to be the same.'

'Yeah.' Ryan drops my hand and starts digging in his jacket pockets. 'I got this thing from the children's centre about the different baby stuff they do. They even have a group for women who are... you know...' He indicates my boobs. '... so I reckon you must be able to find someone else there who likes getting their tits out in public.'

I should probably not repeat that to the group.

'That's wonderful, darling. Thank you.'

I take the leaflet and grin at it.

'What?'

'Nothing.'

'No, come on.'

'Nothing. I just... I love you. With everything that's happened over the past few months, I just... forgot that for a while. I'm sorry.'

He shifts awkwardly. 'Doesn't matter. Sorry, I haven't spent more time here. I just... didn't really seem to be needed.'

'I felt like that a lot too,' I say. 'But I bet we'll miss these days sometimes. When it's 3am, and she's up for the sixth time, I'll probably be wailing, "*Please* bring back the nurses!"'

'Yeah.'

'Not the monitors, though. I never want to see one of those again. At least not unless I also have a sledgehammer.'

'I wonder if I could get an old one on eBay,' Ryan muses. 'Then you actually could smash one to pieces. You could even throw it out the window a couple of times first.'

I laugh. 'Ryan, that's mad!'

'Sorry.'

I take his face between my hands. 'I love that idea. Now kiss me.'

A few days later, I lie in bed in the overnight room, which is also the lounge. It's a sofa bed, and not the most comfortable I've slept in. Next to the bed is Samantha's cot, still firmly fixed to the stand. No monitors. The silence is eery.

She's asleep. I've watched her a bit. Checked her breathing one or twice. Or maybe ten times. But, the truth is, she's never once stopped breathing while she was asleep.

A while later, her cries wake me. I sort a bottle, and she feeds until she's happy. And then I put her back in her cot, and we both go back to sleep. And it's not that scary.

We survive the night.

The next morning, we move back into Samantha's room for another day in Special Care, and suddenly a switch flicks in my brain and it seems ridiculous to be there. We were on our own all night, and it was fine. We were fine. I don't want to endure one more day of hospital life when we don't need to. As wonderful as everyone has been, if I never see this place again it will be too soon.

I get out my phone, call Ryan and tell him to pick us up.

Cassandra comes in while I'm packing up. 'Nearly ready?'

I look around at the wreckage. I hadn't realised quite how much stuff I'd crammed into this little room. 'Little way to go yet. But Ryan won't finish until six, so I have time. How are you feeling?'

'Oh, much better. I'm being referred for counselling as well, so that should help.'

'Wonderful.'

She smiles. 'You know, Tom's moving into Special Care. I think he's getting Samantha's cot.'

'Oh, that's brilliant!' I say, hugging her.

'Yes,' she says. 'You know, I think he's going to be okay.'

When we get home, Ryan carries a sleeping Samantha to his bedroom. Which I guess is *our* bedroom now. And I can't believe the change. For one thing, it's *tidy*. And I think he's actually vacuumed. I didn't even know he *owned* a vacuum.

He's added a dressing table on my side, and on it are the pump, a microwave, the steriliser, a bottle brush, and a fridge for the milk. He's even found me a couple of extra pillows to make sitting up more comfortable. Best of all, he's put her cot on *his side of the bed*. I think that means he's actually planning on getting up when she wakes. It may be the most thoughtful thing he's ever done.

'I love you,' I whisper.

'I love you too,' he whispers back.

Epilogue

Three years later

Samantha is fine. Seriously. Despite me not even making it into the third trimester, there is nothing wrong with her. Her lungs are fine, her eyes are fine, her stomach is fine. And she's beautiful (not just to us, people tell us everywhere we go). Her development is within the normal range for her age. At the later end, admittedly, but it might have been like that anyway. Her size is still below average, but she's slowly catching up. At two, she was discharged from the premature baby clinic at the hospital. Another year or so and you probably won't be able to tell she was early. Don't believe miracles happen? There's one right there.

It took me a while to recover, though. Everyone seemed to assume that things were fine once I'd got her home. That it was just the same as bringing home any newborn. It wasn't. While she was in the hospital, the constant gnawing fear of losing her - plus everything that went on - suppressed most other things. It wasn't until she got home that I really relaxed enough to deal with what had happened. Coming home was only the start.

I went down to pumping part-time when Samantha came home. Fortunately, she took to formula very well.

Actually, I suspect she preferred it. Like that, I managed to push on until she was six months old, which I was quite proud of. Then I stopped. I battled feelings of guilt for a long time, but I can't tell you what a relief it was. Keeping going that long was the hardest thing I have ever done. I think it was almost a penance I imposed on myself to make up for her early arrival, even though rationally I knew it wasn't my fault. If this experience has taught me anything, it's that humans behave very strangely at times.

Ryan and I married the Christmas after she was born. I was quite proud of myself for resisting the pressure to nip down the registry office before then. I wanted to give us time to plan (and slim!) and make the wedding perfect. And it really, really... wasn't. In fact, it all went spectacularly wrong. But, somehow, it didn't matter. And I still think of it as the happiest day of my life.

Meanwhile, my sister has got divorced and my mother has got married and, after a period of adjustment, both are happier than they were before. Amelia still struggles with the "stigma" and has moved to a larger town where everybody doesn't know everybody else's business. Sadly, so has Laura.

After Samantha, I was firmly convinced that I'd never want to risk having another baby. But slowly you forget the pain, and babies start looking cuter. I've just had my implant taken out, so we're officially trying. And I'm terrified. I just hope that, if the worst should happen, I handle it a bit better second time around.

Wish me luck.

THE END

Also by Jennifer Gilby Roberts

The Dr Pepper Prophecies

25-year-old Mel Parker has a few tiny problems:

- Her job is terrible
- She's been dumped yet again
- Her ex is now her boss
- Her parents think she's a loser compared to her perfect younger sister
- All her efforts to improve her life seem doomed to failure
- There just isn't enough chocolate in the world to make up for the above.

The one good thing in her life has always been her best friend Will, who has seen her through every crisis from lost toys to pregnancy scares. But his girlfriend (who's prettier, better-dressed, more successful and secretly evil) is determined to replace Mel as the woman in his life and how is Mel supposed to compete?

So what do you do when you've pretty much given up on your own life? Help others, of course!

After all, what's the worst that can happen?

Also by Jennifer Gilby Roberts

After Wimbledon

After 12 years on the pro. tennis tour and four years with her sort-of boyfriend, Lucy Bennett has had enough. She wants real life... and real love.

Her life, her decision. Right? Well, no one else seems to think so. With opinions on all sides, Lucy's head is spinning. And she's stumbling right into the arms of long-term crush and fellow player Sam. Shame her boyfriend - his arch-rival - would sooner smash a racquet over their heads than agree to a simple change of partners.

As the Wimbledon Championships plays out, Lucy fights for her life on and off the courts. The question is: what will she be left with after Wimbledon?

About Jennifer Gilby Roberts

Jennifer Gilby Roberts has a degree in physics and a postgraduate certificate in computing, so a career writing fiction was inevitable really. She was born and grew up in Surrey/Greater London, but now lives in Richmond, North Yorkshire with her husband, small daughter, two middle-aged cats and a lot of dust bunnies.

Her main job is taking care of her daughter, who was born three months premature but is now a healthy toddler.

She can also be found getting red-faced at zumba class, reading historical porn (as her husband calls it - Regency romance to the rest of us) and humming nursery rhymes while going round Tesco. Her current obsessions include toffee crisp bars, Costa fruit coolers and the TV show *Torchwood.*

Jennifer Gilby Roberts blogs at:
http://jennifergilbyroberts.wordpress.com/

Printed in Great Britain
by Amazon.co.uk, Ltd.,
Marston Gate.